"If you would excuse me then, Lord Giles."

"I'll see you tomorrow."

He bent down to whisper that he would come to get her, and something brushed her cheek. By the time she realized it had been his lips, he was already climbing inside his family's personal carriage, which had followed theirs from the earl's residence.

Giles

Heir to the Earl of Bancroft and scion of House Bancroft, an authoritative noble house that enjoys the trust of the royal family. Handsome and accomplished in both academics and the military. An icy scion who has yet to succumb to any beauty's womanly charms. Goes by both Giles Bancroft and Giles Lowell.

Norman

The youngest child of Baron Hayes. His family has distant ancestral ties to their heirless neighbors, House Clayburn. Intended to marry into House Clayburn, but...

Richard

Son of Marquess Molins and a close friend of Giles. A handsome man who remains single despite extensive experience in the art of romance. Fiona and Giles have entrusted him with their secret plan, but was that wise?

Fiona

Daughter of Baron Clayburn. Works at an art gallery, an unusual choice for a woman of noble birth. Upon learning that her father has been arranging her marriage to a man she has known since childhood, she decides to take her fate into her own hands.

Cecilia

Fiona's little sister. Resembles their late mother. Shy and a bit sickly. Fondly refers to Norman as "Brother."

Hans

An elderly manservant who has served Baron Clayburn's family for years. Loves Fiona and her sister like his own grandchildren. In a bit of a snit about Fiona's sudden romantic interests.

"But you know, Gil, I have an elder brother to hide behind. You, on the other hand, can't run away from marriage forever."

"I'm not comfortable around women."

"I know. Believe me, I do."

Giles sounded as if he had swallowed a lump of lead. Even without seeing his expression, Fiona sensed his sincerity.

Well, this is a surprise. He really is opposed to marriage.

TRUE LOVE
Fades Away When the
Contract Ends

One Star in the Night Sky

WRITTEN BY

Kosuzu Kobato

ILLUSTRATED BY

Fumi Takamura

Airship

Seven Seas Entertainment

Unmei no Koibito wa Kigentsuki Yozora no Hitotsuboshi no Maki Vol. 1
©Kobato Kosuzu (Original Story) ©Fumi Takamura (Illustration)
This edition originally published in Japan in 2023 by
MICRO MAGAZINE, INC., Tokyo.
English translation rights arranged with
MICRO MAGAZINE, INC., Tokyo.

Seven Seas press and purchase enquiries can be sent
to Marketing Manager Lauren Hill at press@gomanga.com.
Information regarding the distribution and purchase of
digital editions is available from Digital Manager CK Russell
at digital@gomanga.com.

Follow Seven Seas Entertainment online at
sevenseasentertainment.com.

TRANSLATION: Julie Goniwich
ADAPTATION: Max Machiavelli
LOGO DESIGN: Mariel Dágá
COVER DESIGN: Nicky Lim
INTERIOR LAYOUT & DESIGN: Clay Gardner
COPY EDITOR: Mark DeJoy
PROOFREADER: Jade Gardner
EDITOR: Laurel Ashgrove
PREPRESS TECHNICIAN: Melanie Ujimori, Jules Valera
MANAGING EDITOR: Alyssa Scavetta
EDITOR-IN-CHIEF: Julie Davis
PUBLISHER: Lianne Sentar
VICE PRESIDENT: Adam Arnold
PRESIDENT: Jason DeAngelis

ISBN: 979-8-88843-759-9
Printed in Canada
First Printing: June 2024
10 9 8 7 6 5 4 3 2 1

Contents

CHAPTER 1

The Rumored Couple

I T WASN'T THE EXQUISITELY decorated hall, the expansive spread of hors d'oeuvres crafted by the esteemed master chef, nor the fancy new gown adorning the earl's only daughter, Caroline, that turned heads at the ball that evening at the Earl of Burleigh's residence.

"Look, over there!"

"Is that Lord Lowell? No, it can't be!"

It was the Viscount Giles Lowell, son of the Earl of Bancroft, and the woman accompanying him that caught everyone's eyes. The two paid no mind to the attention they garnered: They stood close together, each with a glass in hand, never taking their eyes off one another. They were, it seemed, madly in love.

"Oh my, they're so intimate!"

"So, the rumors were true!"

Lord Giles Lowell of House Bancroft—a notorious bachelor, immune to the charms of any woman, whose affections were impossible to win—had at last found his heart's desire. The rumors about his relationship, which had only recently spread through the capital, began with several people claiming to have seen the pair riding in a carriage without a canopy. Before long, these whispers were accompanied by other rumors: "I saw them enjoying an intimate teatime," "I saw them picking out jewelry at Harriet, that high-end boutique..." On and on they went, whirling through the capital's high society just as the social season ramped up.

House Bancroft enjoyed the trust of the royal family. Although it had been engaged in diplomacy for generations, it elected to decline higher titles and remained firmly at the rank of earl. Bancroft possessed a vast domain, and its high status in the peerage was as steadfast as the family's friendships with important people both domestically and abroad.

Giles was the heir to that family. His academic and military accomplishments were common knowledge—and he was handsome, to boot. It was no wonder every eligible woman dreamed to be his wife.

No woman, however, had ever caught the gaze of his grayish-blue eyes. Not once had he shown up to a party or other social gathering with a woman in his company. He had even refused to receive any parties aiming to discuss marriage. Up until now, at twenty-three years old, there had never been a single rumor about him having set his sights on someone. With his perfect looks, chilly appearance, and stoic bearing, he had earned himself the moniker of "the Icy Scion."

None of which was to say that Giles was antisocial: he had plenty of close friends and could even sometimes be seen enjoying pleasant conversations with older women like his godmother, the Marchioness of Heyward. But he always put up a wall between himself and the young ladies. In this way, he was the precise opposite of his best friend, Lord Russel, who everyone knew had already had several romantic entanglements.

And yet Giles's stubbornness—one could almost call it his fastidiousness—only seemed to add to his appeal. The Earl of Burleigh's daughter, Caroline, was first among countless women vying for his heart, and bets were placed every social season as to who would finally win his affections.

Everyone was incredulous when they first heard the rumors that he had found love. And Giles making his first appearance at a party with a woman who wasn't his relative confirmed the rumors at once.

Not only that, but...

"The Icy Scion is actually *smiling*?"

The man rarely showed emotion, yet here he was, beaming at the woman next to him. His smile was so handsome that the cheeks of every nearby woman glowed, except the very woman he was smiling at: she carried on chatting with him like his expression was a mundane, everyday occurrence.

"Say, do you know her?"

"She seldom comes to our parties. I believe she's the daughter of Baron Clayburn."

"Clayburn? Oh, that nobleman who lives out in the country."

The woman in question was as plain as the subdued color of her gown. The rumors held that she was Fiona Clayburn, the elusive eighteen-year-old daughter of Baron Clayburn who only stayed in the capital for brief stints during each social season. Given her rare attendance at parties, few in the capital knew her by sight.

She was ordinary-looking, anyway, and not the type to leave a lasting impression. What did draw everyone's attention, however, was the beautiful, glittering ring on her left hand.

"That yellow diamond! It's so beautiful!"

"They're truly engaged, then?"

"I can't believe such a plain girl would be the one to win Lord Giles's heart."

The young ladies who had hoped to be Giles's wife clenched their teeth as they glared at Fiona. It was common for Giles to merely show his face at parties before making a prompt exit; the fact that he was here now as a proper escort, never leaving Fiona's side for a moment, further fueled the flames of jealousy.

Giles paused his conversation to elegantly lift Fiona's hand and bring his lips to the finger that bore the diamond ring. The sight of this sparked a shrill commotion from the jealous on-lookers, and some brave soul chose that moment to intrude upon Giles and Fiona's private world.

"My, my, look how intimate you two are." It was Lord Richard Russel, Giles's best friend and the son of the Marquess of Molins. Handsome like Giles, but jovial where Giles was cold, Richard was popular with the high society crowd. The sight of both hand-some young lords in such close proximity was enough to make the women present swoon.

Richard smiled as he approached, but Giles's answering smile did not meet his eyes. "I didn't know you were here, Rick."

"I got here long before you two. I waited for you, but as you didn't seem to notice, I decided to come over and interrupt." With one smooth motion, Richard captured Fiona's slender hand from Giles, causing further commotion from onlookers as he kissed the back of it. "Good evening, Miss Clayburn. I hope you are enjoying the ball?"

"Yes, thank you. I hope you are as—oh!"

Giles swiftly reclaimed her hand. The plain look of displeasure on his usually impassive face served yet another shock to their audience.

"Now, now," Richard admonished. "Women don't like men who are overly possessive."

"Mind your own business," Giles retorted.

Richard basked in Giles's scowl as he plucked the glass from Fiona's other hand. Then he cast a meaningful glance toward the dancefloor. "Since you're here and all, you should go dance."

Giles gave it a moment of thought. "That's a good idea. Come, Fiona." He placed his own glass on a passing servant's tray and took Fiona's hand. "If you would excuse us, Lord Russel."

"I'll catch up with you again later. Go have fun." Richard waved as Fiona and Giles made their way to the center of the hall. Within moments, he was swarmed by women.

"Why, Lord Richard! Do you know her?"

"How long have they been together? Are the rumors all true?"

The ladies were pushy, their eyes gleaming as they tried to get to the bottom of things.

"Just between you and me..." Richard lowered his voice with a hint of amusement, "it all began during the celebration for the prince's debut the other day." He testified that he had been there when Fiona and Giles first met.

The ladies agreed that if Giles's best friend said so, then it must be true. Once his back was turned, however, they ridiculed her.

"That girl is not attractive in the least."

"Lady Caroline would make a far more suitable match."

At that remark, Caroline hid a smirk behind her folding fan. It was vexing for the man she had her eyes on to attend *her* party with another woman on his arm, especially a woman of lower status and appearance. While Fiona's house—the house of Baron Clayburn—was indeed an old family, that was all she had going for her. Her family carried no influence, nor was her father employed at a major post. What's more, standing next to Giles, it was clear he was out of Fiona's league.

With her fan clenched in her hand, Caroline glared at the sight of them happily dancing a waltz. "How could he have picked someone like her over me?" she fumed and then walked away.

Richard looked askance at the women who hurried along in her wake and granted a charming smile to those who remained behind. "As it so happens, there was a bit of an accident. That was how they fell for one another."

"What kind of accident?"

"They say it's the secret of lovers... In other words, fate brought them together." One of his pretty blue eyes closed in a wink, inciting another round of shrieks.

"He said it's fate!"

"I suppose it would have to be, for Lord Giles to fall in love."

The women chattered excitedly, declaring it to be like something out of a novel or a play. Satisfied that they were beginning to accept his story, Richard nodded and then raised his glass high. "To lovers."

He toasted in the direction of the new couple, who were dancing intimately with one another. After a pause, Giles said to Fiona, "It's really having an effect. Now do you believe me?"

"Yes. You and Rick were right. I underestimated how powerful rumors can be."

Satisfied, Fiona smiled as Giles wrapped his arm around her back, drawing her closer. Their feet were already brushing against one another as they performed the dance steps, but now they were close enough that their knees touched as well. Fiona nearly stumbled, but Giles steadied her and corrected her position.

"I-it's hard to dance when we're this close."

"He told us to stick close together, didn't he?"

"But there's a limit to that."

"There is? It's hard to tell how far I should go." Gazing into one another's eyes so closely, they certainly looked like a couple whispering sweet nothings to each other.

From a distance, with Giles's dark blond hair sparkling from the light of the chandelier, it must have seemed as if his grayish-blue eyes were gazing adoringly at his beloved. But having spent the past few days with him, Fiona understood what that look was: those were the eyes of a scoundrel.

She didn't mind his elation at seeing his plan succeed, but it wouldn't do for him to expose them during their public debut as a couple. Fiona decided that a stern warning was in order. "Don't distract me with your teasing. I'm not very good at dancing."

"Get used to it, then. This will be the first of many dances."

Fiona's eyes briefly widened at this indication that he did not intend to refrain from touching her, but she quickly regained her composure. "Might you accompany me as I practice, then?" she retorted.

"My beloved's wish is my command."

Fiona averted her gaze to hide her shock. After a moment she asked, "You know what you just said, right?"

Giles was looking into the distance, but an amused smile tugged at his lips.

This display of another rare smile from Giles caused a small commotion amongst their onlookers. Several women stormed out of the hall in sheer indignation. Noticing this out of the corner of their eyes, Fiona and Giles exchanged a look.

"It's working faster than I anticipated. By the way, Lord Giles, don't forget that it should be 'my fake beloved.'"

"Ah, my apologies. This is the first time I've enjoyed a party this much. I got a bit carried away."

Had anyone seen up close, they would have realized that the feeling with which they gazed into one another's eyes was not ardent love at all but solidarity. Fortunately, the crowd now maintained a wide berth around the "fervent lovers," so no one was close enough to discover the truth.

"I say this again: I'll be counting on you this season, Fiona," Giles said. With the music approaching its conclusion, he stolidly twirled Fiona into her final turn.

Their linked hands were outstretched so that everyone could get a good view of the sparkling ring. Fiona lifted her skirts for a graceful curtsy. "I shall do my best to play the part of your lover, Lord Giles."

Fiona and Giles first met on the night of the celebration of the prince's birth. Nobles had gathered at the palace to honor the infant prince; there was an extraordinary turnout.

The prince, who had yet to reach his first birthday, was introduced to all in attendance, after which point the celebration was like any other evening party. As it was hosted by the royal family, however, the food served and the partygoers' attire were even more lavish than usual.

All the palace's gardens, not just the biggest one, were open to visitors that night. Many of the beautifully attired guests slipped out of the great hall to seek refuge in them. Even the smaller gardens were much bigger than the main ones at the nobles' townhouses, and lanterns brightly illuminated the spaces, lending them a kind of beauty not seen during the daytime. They were

furnished with tables and benches so that people could enjoy food and drink while they conversed.

Though it was nighttime, guards and servants patrolled the gardens, making it perfectly safe for young women to enjoy the scenery while enjoying a good chat. Among them was a young woman who walked through the gardens without giving a single glance to the perfectly symmetrical beds of flowers or the intricate water fountains.

Fiona, who was in attendance with her father, Baron Clayburn, cast her eyes down as she sighed. "This isn't fun at all." She was well-mannered in the way she covered her mouth with her half-closed fan. Her dull blonde hair and amber-colored eyes were both common colors in this land, and she wore an under-stated gown with minimal accessories. Of average height and with unremarkable looks, she was not the kind of woman who stood out in a crowd, and she was outshone by her resplendent surroundings as she walked.

But Fiona had something on her mind. It was a serious and extremely private matter. She hadn't even told much to Olga, her best friend and daughter of Viscount Symonds. She especially could not tell her younger sister, with whom she was close. This was something that she had been anguishing over alone for some time now.

I was hoping that coming here would get my mind off things, but it's not working. Tonight was a rare opportunity: a mere daughter of a baron, like her, was permitted entrance to the palace. She had hoped that being surrounded by the splendor of the palace and all its beautiful paintings and sculptures would lift her spirits, but none of it was helping her feel any better. Instead, she had accidentally stepped on the foot of a boy she had known since she was young, and she could barely pay attention when her best friend talked to her. Fiona's gloomy expression was a damper on the evening for her friends, who had been hoping to enjoy this rare opportunity to the fullest.

She slipped away from her companions, who were enjoying the food and dancing, and found her father chatting with an acquaintance. She whispered in his ear, "I'm going to go see the garden," before leaving the lively great hall.

She sought quiet in the small garden but there were more people there than she anticipated. A sense that she alone felt melancholy among the jovial partygoers made her even more depressed. Fiona gave a small sigh and headed for a place where she could be alone. *Two more weeks until the party for my engagement announcement...*

Weighing heavily on Fiona's heart was her engagement to Norman Hayes, whom she had known since she was young. He had been negotiating their betrothal behind closed doors.

It had all started because heavy rains flooded the river at the border of their families' fiefs. The bridge washed away, and it was going to take a considerable sum of money to repair the riverbank. Though the families shared common ancestors and their fiefs bordered one another, the difference in how the repair costs impacted each house was like the difference between heaven and earth: House Hayes enjoyed considerable wealth and could easily obtain fine lumber, whereas House Clayburn was just scraping along.

After discussing the distribution of their contributions, House Hayes agreed to shoulder the bulk of the cost. There was a condition, however: Norman would marry into House Clayburn and become the heir to Baron Clayburn, who only had two daughters, Fiona and Cecilia.

This discussion was kept between her father and Baron Hayes—Fiona was told nothing of it. She learned of the plan only because she happened to overhear one of their conversations when they left a door slightly ajar.

"The two of them do get along quite well," she heard Baron Hayes suggest.

"That's true, though she is a tomboy," her father answered.

"That's not a problem at all. If anything, my son is spoiled from being the youngest. He can be a bit unreliable at times, but I think that's all the more reason why Fiona would make an excellent match for him."

Fiona could not believe her ears. It was a wonder that she didn't drop the bundle of documents she had been carrying. *Yes, we get along because we've known each other for years now, but I'm still not ready for marriage!*

Fiona was eighteen, which was a normal age for marriage. If anything, she was late in finding herself a fiancé. However, Fiona wasn't like the other daughters of the peerage—she worked. She was her uncle's assistant because she wanted to do the job. Her father tolerated it, but she would be forced to quit the moment she was married—although they were mere countryside nobles, it would wound the family's reputation if word got out that the wife of a nobleman had a job.

I don't want to quit. Not to mention, marrying Norman? I can't do it. I simply cannot imagine it.

They had played together as children since before she could remember, always getting covered in mud. While he was a man now, she could only see Norman as a brother. In fact, she thought of him like a younger brother even though he was a year older. The two of them would argue about anything and everything. Perhaps in their fathers' eyes it looked like they got along, but that wasn't the case.

"Then let's announce their engagement at the capital after the start of the season," Baron Hayes continued.

"Ha ha ha! Let's keep it a secret from Fiona and enjoy the look of shock on her face when we announce it!" her father conspired.

Fiona choked back a scream. *I can't believe them! Who would ever enjoy that kind of surprise?!*

If she ran away from home, it would only give way to misunderstandings about her being bashful about the whole thing. In fact, letting them know that she knew what was going on would likely make them speed up their plans. Their fathers were not being malicious, though—they believed that Fiona would be happy about the engagement. The problem was...she wasn't.

She had staggered down a step and sat down, which was poor behavior on her part, and held her head wearily. Not the type to dwell on her troubles for long, she thought, *I need to talk to*

Norman about this. Fiona stood then, filled with determination, and went searching for him.

She quickly found Norman by a flower bed in the garden with her younger sister, Cecilia.

"Norman, come here for a minute, would you?"

"Whoa, don't scare me like that."

"Just come on! Cecilia, I'm going to be borrowing him for a few minutes."

"A-all right?"

She dragged Norman out of sight of her confused sister. The reason Norman didn't try to shake Fiona's grip on his hand, despite his protests, was because they were friends—*not* because he was in love with her. Fiona stopped near the elm tree at the edge of the garden, where Norman calmly asked, "Has something happened?"

"You won't believe what I just heard!"

Norman was objectively an attractive man, even as he looked at her in puzzlement. He had slightly wavy golden hair and clear brown eyes. The colorful hues of his features gave the impression of a good-natured dog that would harm neither man nor beast.

Norman didn't bother to brace himself as he waited for Fiona to explain. "They're talking about marrying us," she said bluntly. "Did you know about this?"

"Ah. So it's happening, huh?"

Fiona was stunned at his nonchalant response. She grabbed his arms and started shaking him. "Wh-what do you mean? So you *did* know about it? This means we're actually going to be married!"

"You mean to tell me that you didn't know?" His response flustered Fiona. Norman's smile was one of resignation as he peeled Fiona's hands off his arms. "You never stopped to wonder why only I ever came over, or why I travel around your fief with your father?"

"Huh?" Fiona was stunned.

It was true that it was always Norman alone who came to their home to play; his older brothers seldom visited. Furthermore, Norman had started working as her father's secretary recently, which meant that he regularly accompanied her father on inspections of their fief and in meetings with neighboring lords.

"Since it's just me and my sister, I thought that you might inherit our property... But I never thought that might include marriage of all things!"

"I had assumed the same, but it seems we were both wrong."

"Huh? Wait, but..."

Only men could inherit, and in families with only daughters, it was common to adopt a son into the house to be the heir. Marriage wasn't a necessary part of the process. Until recently, Fiona's father had never spoken a word to her about marriage, let alone wanting her to get engaged. This was why she assumed that he planned to adopt Norman without marrying them.

Fiona was in a panic over the situation, but neither Norman's expression nor his tone was any different from usual. "I don't mind marrying you," he said. "There's no reason to worry about us potentially getting married."

"I don't remember ever having once worried about you in my whole life."

"That's true, I feel like there never was a need for you to worry about me to begin with."

His response was nonchalant, but she couldn't laugh with him like normal. In fact, the way she pouted made him laugh all the more.

"It'll be fine, right? I'm just going to start living here and things will be the same between us as they always have been."

She had good reason to think so. She and Norman had grown up together, since before her earliest memories, and they were even distant relatives. That meant they were already family. Still, the thought of them formally becoming husband and wife was hard for Fiona to swallow.

After a short pause, she asked, "Do you have someone you're in love with?"

"I'm not sure. I've never thought about it before. But I'm guessing you don't."

Fiona bit back her rebuttal and held her head in her hands. "Aaaagh! This is all happening because of the river."

"Huh? No, it's not. You were talking about how you plan to go abroad with Uncle Reggie next year, weren't you? Your father is more worried about that than the whole business about the construction."

"What?" Uncle Reginald was the man she worked for. He lived his life on the road, traveling between other countries and their home country. Fiona grew up listening to his tales of all the different countries of the world, so it was natural that she wanted to see them with her own eyes.

She had asked him about it, and he promised to take her when she became an adult. That was three years ago, and next year she would finally be old enough. Fiona was counting down the days in anticipation of it.

"They said that if you get married, then you'll have to stay here." Norman lowered his voice, sounding a bit hesitant. "You know they're worried because of what happened to Auntie."

"Oh, yes..."

Fiona's mother had died the year after she gave birth to Cecilia. With her weak constitution, she was unable to fully recover from childbirth. Fiona was like her father not only in looks but in constitution: she was so healthy that she hardly ever caught a cold. It had never occurred to her that her own conduct might be cause for concern in light of her mother's death. Nor had her uncle—her mother's younger brother—ever said a word about it.

But it was clear her father felt differently.

"B-but Father said I could go."

Norman smiled crookedly. "Well, I'm guessing he did so because you claimed it would be for the sake of the fief."

Sightseeing and assisting her uncle weren't the only reasons Fiona wanted to travel—she also wanted to do it for their fief. The Barony of Clayburn was good land, full of simple and beautiful landscapes and quiet people. However, they didn't have any special resources, places, or products that could bring tourism. As a result, the family was barely making ends meet.

They needed funds to bring doctors to their clinics, teachers to their schools, and to plant new kinds of crops. The recent flood wasn't the first natural disaster to befall them either. It had been recommended that they make some investments, but that required having capital on hand to begin with. Besides, with their lack of connections to high society, it would be difficult to know what to invest in. Fiona hoped, if possible, to find a sound and steady source of funds in her travels. With that reasoning, her father had agreed, despite the somewhat perplexed frown he wore.

"The truth is that he doesn't want you to go," Norman continued.

Revitalizing their fief was always a topic of discussion. If anything, her father should've welcomed her proposal. But, as Norman revealed to Fiona, her father couldn't help but worry that something might happen to her, or that she might fall ill, while she was in a foreign land.

"To be honest, your father was able to come up with the funds without my family's help. He petitioned the Crown's treasury for a loan because of the scope of the damage and the construction required to repair it. So I think that you're actually to blame for our future marriage."

Fiona was so astounded to learn that the reason for these sudden talks of marriage partially lay with her that all she could say was, "N-no!"

"Sister? Norman? Um, are you finished with your conversation?" Cecilia gently interrupted as she approached.

"Oh, yes, Cecilia. It's all right now." Fiona, who was clutching her head at this shocking revelation, raised it at her sister's timid voice.

"I'm sorry for interrupting. I came to get you because they said the pie has finished baking."

"My, that sounds wonderful. Thanks for letting us know." Norman grinned at news of his favorite food, causing a scarlet bloom in Cecilia's cheeks.

"Oh, uh, you're welcome."

Cecilia was shy because she was prone to sickness and lived her whole life inside the confines of the estate. She was especially unsure of how to act around men. Despite growing up with Norman as much as Fiona, still she acted like this, so Fiona assumed that her sister was just shy with everyone. *But surely...*

Norman understood Cecilia's personality. And it went without saying that their father couldn't bear the thought of his youngest daughter growing up. Most importantly, Cecilia herself wasn't aware of it. *If he wants to marry Norman into our family so badly, then there's a more suitable choice for his bride.*

Fiona made Norman promise that he wouldn't tell her father that she had overheard; she was all but certain he would make the announcement sooner if he knew. *I need to buy myself as much time as possible to come up with a plan.*

Time passed, however, and she had not had a chance to consult with Norman. Now here she was, in the capital. Norman was also here at the prince's celebration, but they could neither discuss the matter in front of so many people nor come up with a good plan in the short course of a dance.

She was stuck.

The construction work for the river had begun. Their fathers were likely to announce their engagement at the party scheduled in half a month's time at the Clayburn estate. Besides, even if she did manage to avoid marrying Norman, her father was sure to find her another match if he was dead set against the idea of her traveling. And then next year, there would be the marriage ceremony just before she became an adult.

I do love Father. I understand that he's worried about me. But...

She wanted to see more of the vast world with her own eyes. She wanted to work and make her own living. And she absolutely hated the idea of being a caged bird who had to rely on someone else.

Fiona also understood that her way of thinking was not accepted by society. She also knew that her father secretly planned to marry her to Norman because he wished for her happiness. She was at a loss for what to do and the more she agonized over it, the more disturbing her ideas became.

"Perhaps I have no choice but to run away."

As these dangerous words slipped out of her mouth, she came back to her senses. *Huh? Where am I?* She had walked for so long, staring at her feet, that she now found herself in a place devoid of people. She looked around in a panic and discovered an aged brick wall up ahead with a wooden door—the end of the garden.

Fiona was surprised to have come so far in shoes she was unaccustomed to wearing. Standing still for a moment, she realized how tired she was. She looked around some more and saw a lattice cloaked in white-flowered vines. Before it was a garden bench with delicate cabriole legs. *Surely, it will be okay if I rest here for a bit...*

There were sure to be guards on patrol, even if she didn't see any other guests. The lanterns were also brightly lit; besides, she was in a castle. There couldn't be any dangers lurking here. When Fiona sat down on the bench, the sweet fragrance of the small blooming flowers behind her flooded her senses. As she sighed in relief at the smell of the flowers, it happened...

"I told you already, I have no interest in getting married."

"You know you're not getting out of it, Gil."

Fiona heard the voices of two men behind her. She couldn't see them because of the dense greenery, but it seemed there was another bench just on the other side of the lattice. She could feel the vibration as they sat down on it.

"I would sooner become a volunteer soldier and go abroad."

"The next time you do go, it'll be as a diplomat. With your wife in tow, of course."

"Give me a break. There'd be no point in even going then."

She heard the sound of one man lightly patting the other's shoulder as he laughed with absolute displeasure. He didn't sound amiable at all.

"It's not my concern, Rick."

"Now, now, Gil. You've got the weight of the entire house of the Earl of Bancroft resting on your shoulders. It'll be no surprise to me if your father and the others force you into it."

Gil from the family of the Earl of Bancroft? And Rick... Wait, could they be Giles Bancroft and Richard Russel? Fiona was stunned by the names she overheard. On the other side of the lattice were two people who were very famous in high society.

The moodily grumbling "Gil" must be Lord Giles Lowell, the heir to the Earl of Bancroft, a senior statesman. Lord Lowell had lovely dark blond hair and smoky grayish-blue eyes. His cool, handsome features and prestigious pedigree on both sides made him the ideal suitor in the eyes of many young ladies.

And Rick, the friend who was trying to pacify him, was surely Lord Richard Russel. The two of them were best friends of the same age and Fiona had heard that they were often together. Lord Russel was the third son of the Marquess of Molins and Fiona's impression was that he was the sort of person who always had a smile on his face. His hair was a bright honey blond, and he was handsome too, but in the opposite way from Giles—gentler, or so Fiona had heard.

These two were famous enough that even Fiona, who kept herself uninvolved with the goings-on in high society, had heard of them. And right now, the only thing separating her from them was this lattice.

Right, Olga was all excited because she passed them by in the corridor earlier. I can't believe I've come across them too. I guess that's a party at the royal palace for you.

Even though they were all labeled as nobles, they were from different worlds due to the difference in status and sex. In fact, Fiona had never even seen the two with her own eyes before.

Recalling what her gossip-loving best friend had told her, she was certain that they must be five years older than her eighteen-year-old self. As she was calculating that on her fingers, she heard yet another sigh.

"My parents are bad enough as it is, but even my relatives won't get off my back. It's becoming a real nuisance."

"Hey, you wouldn't want any of them to overhear you now."

"Nobody ever comes all the way over here."

Though Fiona hadn't intended it, she was eavesdropping. She knew she should leave but given that marriage was the root of Fiona's troubles as well, the topic of their conversation had piqued her interest.

Did he just say that he has no interest in marriage? Same as me. However...

Succeeding a house was a noble's most important duty. The Bancrofts had been leaders among the nobility ever since the founding of their nation. In particular, they were appointed to the post of foreign affairs. Their earldom was located along the coast and had a trade port, making them a point of contact for commerce between other countries.

As the next head of the family, Giles would need a partner no matter what. He could remain unmarried and choose to adopt a child instead, but his parents and relatives were sure to object. Their affairs were completely different from those of Fiona's family, who sat snugly at the lowest rank of the peerage.

Ideas came to Fiona one after the other, but she was pulled from her reverie by the sound of Richard's voice.

"Maybe you should just mess around then? You never know, they might even get off your back out of disgust, like my family has with me."

Oh, yes, that's right. Lord Russel is known for his long history of love affairs.

He was a famous philanderer, and she would need both hands and feet to count the number of women, young and old, with whom he had carried on affairs. There were also rumors of countless lovers he had known but for a single night. It was incredible, even if it was all exaggerated.

I could never behave as Lord Russel does, though, so that idea won't do.

She had never heard of any conflict arising from it, so whatever took place between him and his lovers must have been by mutual agreement, but Fiona found it a bit hard to comprehend. Not that she really cared that much—they were his affairs, not hers.

"You know, Rick, I'm worried that they're going to pin you down too before long."

"Don't worry. I've already picked someone out."

"Don't brag."

It appeared that Giles held the same opinion as Fiona. Richard was laughing cheerfully, but Fiona could tell even through the lattice that Giles must be wearing a scowl.

"But you know, Gil, I have an elder brother to hide behind. You, on the other hand, can't run away from marriage forever."

"I'm not comfortable around women."

"I know. Believe me, I do."

Giles sounded as if he had swallowed a lump of lead. Even without seeing his expression, Fiona sensed his sincerity.

Well, this is a surprise. He really is opposed to marriage.

Unlike women, men had a lengthy window within which they were considered to be of marriageable age. They had the luxury to pick and choose, so Fiona had assumed Giles was being careful in choosing his future bride, but it seemed she was wrong.

From the other side of the lattice, she heard him grumble about how practically every day he received letters of introductions and invitations as his relatives attempted to arrange prospective choices for his bride. "Just the night before last, I arrived home to find a woman I had never seen before at my house. I really wish they would cut it out already."

"Oh? The work of that aunt of yours again, I imagine? Anyway, what happened with your uninvited guest?"

"I asked her to leave at once."

"I had a feeling. Sorry you had to deal with that."

Wow, that's awful.

Forcibly sending someone of the opposite sex to someone's home was simply taking matchmaking too far. This aunt of his must have resorted to such methods because she was worried about the earl's lineage, but surely it would only backfire when sprung on someone who was against the idea of marriage in the first place.

"Is tonight's party helping you feel even a little better?"

"No, not at all."

I understand. I truly, deeply understand how you feel. She began to feel an affinity with Giles after hearing he wasn't having a good time at the celebration either.

The men continued their conversation. It almost felt like they were trying to let Fiona overhear as she began to agree with Giles wholeheartedly.

"Ha ha. I guess it makes sense, since the girls were swarming around you. It was quite the spectacle."

"It's not funny."

"It's your fault for coming to this party alone. You should have just picked a random girl to bring."

Apparently, he typically brought his older sister with him to parties, but since she was married off to the Marquess of Colet, he was forced to attended parties alone. Again, Fiona knew this courtesy of Olga.

"I can't think of a single woman I could invite who wouldn't get the wrong idea."

"Neither can I. But that's why I tried to help you out back there. Don't be mad at me." Richard pointed out that Giles had left himself wide open, but a gust of wind blew past, and Fiona couldn't make out Giles's reply.

Off in the distance, she heard the voices of several women. They were still far away enough that she couldn't make out what they were saying, but they seemed to be heading in the direction of Fiona, Giles, and Richard.

The small garden was lovely, but the only thing that really stood out was the fountain by the entrance. There was nothing

of interest to young women back here. Which could only mean...
Did those girls come here chasing after these two?

Listening closely, she heard a girl claim she saw Lord Giles
come this way. Fiona's guess had been right: these must be the
girls from whom Giles and Richard had sought refuge.

She should probably let them know the girls were coming
as a means of apology for her unintended eavesdropping. While
she didn't feel any better about her current dilemma, discovering
someone who could sympathize with her in her disinterest in
marriage lifted Fiona's mood somewhat.

*Uh, okay, just act casual, like you just happened to be passing
by now.*

Fiona stood up from the bench.

CHAPTER 2

Encounter

"**G**OOD EVENING. It's such a wonderful night, don't you agree?" Fiona moved to stand before the two of them, pretending she just happened to be passing by. She gathered her skirts as she gave a simple curtsy. Her conduct was most natural; Richard's expression and mannerisms changed while Giles turned to ice. Each stood up to return her curtsy with a bow, but only Richard spoke.

"What a pretty lady you are. Are you having a good time tonight?"

"Oh, yes, very much so." *Wow. Just as I would have expected. He told me I'm pretty so smoothly.*

While Fiona's sister was a dead ringer for their beautiful mother, Fiona had their father's ordinary looks. Richard was merely being cordial, using the compliment as a springboard for polite conversation. Understanding as much, Fiona smiled and carried on in the same nonchalant tone. "I was so taken by the garden that I accidentally found myself here at the end of it."

"Why, that's how we found ourselves here as well." Richard was used to dealing with people—women in particular—so she didn't sense even a hint of aversion from him. In fact, she was astonished at how eloquently he spoke.

These sorts of parties always had many attendees who had yet to be introduced to one another. While it was good manners to exchange greetings when meeting a fellow partygoer for the first time, after that point it was up to the interlocutors to decide whether or not to continue the conversation.

Fiona's smiled deepened as she pretended not to notice that Giles was on edge. He came seeking a reprieve from the young ladies who had swarmed him, after all. "Um, I just thought you should know that—"

Her warning was interrupted by a high-pitched voice. "Lord Giles! How could you go and hide from us like this?"

Huh? How'd she get here so fast? Fiona was stunned. She had been certain she still had time before Giles's pursuers reached them, but here came a woman from behind Fiona, intent on reaching Giles. Richard made an utterance of surprise, and Giles's blank look grew a shade chillier.

"You there," said the woman. "Step aside."

"Ah!" Fiona was feeling guilty for not warning the young lords in time when the woman shoved her in the back—and it was clearly not by accident. Caught off guard, Fiona lost her balance and toppled over.

Giles, who happened to be standing in front of her, caught her slim body snugly in his arms.

What the—?!

Fiona's cheek pressed against the elegant fabric of his jacket. Giles's arms looked slender, but they were surprisingly strong; he had no trouble supporting her. She had avoided falling on her face, but now she was wrapped up in his embrace.

She looked up at him in surprise, and with hardly any distance between them, his grayish-blue eyes met her gaze. Those eyes were as cold and emotionless as starlight. Fiona blinked a few times as she stared into them.

Wow, he has such a pretty face. Like one of Lucefarna's sculptures. Seeing Giles's face up close like this for the very first time, Fiona was surprised to find that his handsome features reminded her of a marble statue she had seen at an art museum. Only when his eyes colored over with a hint of displeasure did she realize that she was still staring, and should come back to herself.

"M-my sincerest apologies."

"No need to apologize. Are you all right?"

"Huh?"

Giles had just complained at length about his discomfort with women. She assumed that he must detest being in direct contact with her like this, even if it was an accident, so his concern for her well-being took Fiona off guard. *Oh, of course. He's simply being a gentleman and minding his manners.*

He must have protected her out of reflex, thanks to his upbringing as a gentleman. Being well-bred certainly had its good points as well as its bad.

"Um, yes. I'm fi—ow!" Fiona tried to put her weight on her own two feet, but a throbbing pain shot up her leg from her right ankle, making her grimace.

"Is something the matter?"

"Oh, no, I'm fine."

She knew she must have sprained it in the fall, but informing him of her injury would land her in the doctor's room, and the whole situation would create a fuss. This was the prince's special day; she didn't want to ruin the mood by causing a scene with her injury.

Instead, she smiled and tried to hide the dull pain in her foot. Just before she could thank him again, the same shrill voice pierced the air from behind her.

"Where are your manners? How long do you intend to cling to him?"

"But you were—" *the one who pushed me,* Fiona turned and began to object. But before she could finish the sentence, she was met by a legion of young women who glared at her, complaining.

Uh-huh, uh-huh. I get it. I'm in your way. These women had no intention of admitting they were at fault or even listening to what she had to say. The will to argue drained out of her. The crowd took advantage of Fiona's hesitation to push her aside, properly this time, and close in on Giles and Richard.

I might as well just go now. Her hope was to warn them before these women arrived, but it was too late, and now there was no point in Fiona being there. She curtsied with a small sigh; sure, no one was looking, but it wouldn't do to forget her manners.

As Fiona turned away, one of the men called out to her, "Oh, wait!" But Fiona was too focused on the pain in her foot to notice.

On her way back to the hall, she spotted her father on the promenade, headed her way. She waved to catch his attention, and he trotted over to her.

"I'm glad I managed to catch you, my dear. I know it's early yet, but I thought we should head out now, before the roads become crowded with everyone else leaving. Oh my—what's happened to your foot?"

"I sprained it. I'm just not used to walking in such high heels." Fiona spun a lie about how she was so taken with the garden that she forgot to pay attention to her feet. She also assured him that it didn't hurt much.

"That's even more reason for us to hurry home, then. And here I had thought you were finally starting to act a bit more ladylike. Let me guess, you were looking at something while you were walking? Or did you decide to try running?"

"No, nothing of the sort. This is the *palace*, after all."

"No? Then were you climbing a tree?"

"Father!"

"Ha ha ha, I jest."

Fiona resembled her father even more when they both smiled. Passersby grinned fondly at the friendly quarrel.

"Let us be off then, Father. I'm sure that Cecilia is still awake, awaiting our return."

"I'm sure you're right."

Fiona took her father's arm. They reached their carriage before long, and not a moment too soon: Fiona's throbbing ankle was just starting to feel hot. She sighed as she sat down in her seat. *This is certainly one way for me to get my mind off things.* Sure, none of her troubles had been solved, but now she could only focus on the pain.

She had been kicked and trampled on, but for some reason, her heart actually felt lighter. Perhaps she was just happy to have found an ally in her feelings about marriage, one-sided as the association may be. *To think that even a man as blessed as Giles has his worries.* He was a future earl, he had a keen mind, and he was attractive. Feeling even this small kinship with a man who shone brightest among the glittering stars made her smile in spite of herself.

Perhaps it's too early to give up.

Her deadline was half a month away. Or, if she thought of it another way, she still had half a month to figure things out. Her uncle's response to her letter requesting help was due to arrive soon too. Perhaps he would have advice for her.

Fiona's head was resting against the small window of the rumbling carriage when her father asked, "Did you manage to make any new acquaintances tonight?"

"Acquaintances?" She thought of the women she met in the small garden. Those women were less like acquaintances and more like hunters seeking their prey. "Not really... I did speak a bit with someone, but no one quite like Olga." Fiona straightened her posture and smiled wryly as she said her friend's name. "They were all such elegant ladies that I lost my nerve."

"Is that so? Well, I suppose it makes sense. This is the capital, after all."

Fiona didn't introduce herself to any of them, but they were sure to be of higher rank than herself. They all wore such opulent dresses, and their self-confidence was palpable from the way they behaved. *Definitely not the type of women you'd find back home.*

As a nobleman from the countryside, Baron Clayburn did not have many connections. The only aristocrats with whom they socialized were old acquaintances. If anything, Fiona mingled more with people who were not members of the peerage these days.

Olga didn't care about rank, or perhaps it was more accurate to say she was easygoing. Unlike the women Fiona encountered in the garden, Olga had no designs of marrying up in rank.

It was uncommon in their society for a noblewoman to want to work and be independent. Women's lives revolved around marriage; it was drilled into them from infancy that they must procure an advantageous match for the sake of themselves and their families. Everyone around them supported this notion, saying it was the only way to find happiness. Given their upbringing, the way the young ladies in the garden had behaved made sense.

But Fiona couldn't help thinking differently.

Affection for someone chosen for you depended on the conditions under which they had been chosen. Perhaps other people didn't mind being matched up, but it felt purposeless if politics or money were the only reason for the marriage.

Of course, it wasn't enough to be in love either. Fiona knew this, but she felt that what a person was like on the inside was just as important as their rank or appearance. This was one reason Fiona objected to her imminent engagement.

Not after growing up listening to Father's tales of Mother.

She knew that they had been a loving couple; her father had deeply loved her mother. Many encouraged him to find a new wife after Fiona's mother passed, but he remained a widower. Fiona wanted, if at all possible, to find a similar match: a partner with whom she had an emotional connection.

All those young ladies at the party seemed to unilaterally seek a husband out without putting any thought into his circumstances or feelings about the matter. It would be ironic if it turned out that the reason Giles balked at the thought of marriage was because of how aggressive such women were.

He held me so closely. Fiona had felt so secure in his embrace. With a steady grip like that, she supposed it must be true that he was skilled with a blade.

Recalling the moment now brought the sensation of his touch vividly to mind. They really had been close. Closer than when dancing with a partner. She had rarely ever been touched by a member of the opposite sex at that proximity. Aside from her father, the last time she could recall such an event was when she hugged her uncle goodbye before he left on his travels.

Remembering the warmth of Giles's touch caused a responding heat to bloom in Fiona's cheeks—even now, well after the fact.

She raised her hand to fan herself. As she did so, she noticed that something was caught in the cuff of her sleeve.

"Hmm?" In the dim light of the carriage, she gently removed a short chain caught on her lace. *Did this catch when he grabbed me?* She recalled seeing something that looked similar on Giles's wrist in the garden.

"What is it?" Fiona's father asked.

"Oh, nothing. I'm just a bit tired now."

"I'll wake you when we arrive, so feel free to get some rest."

"Thank you, Father."

She shut her eyes, pretending to sleep. In her hand she grasped the onyx cuff link. It was the color of the night sky outside the window—a cuff link that bore the crest of the earl's house.

Cecilia saw through Fiona's deflections about her ankle from the very moment Fiona arrived home.

"Don't worry, Cecilia, I can take care of it myself."

"Nonsense. You sit right there. Hans, please bring the medicine box."

Before Fiona could stop him, the family's elderly manservant brought the medicine box and applied a poultice of soaked arnica to her ankle. The cool poultice felt nice on her hot ankle, and Fiona sighed in relief.

Cecilia skillfully wrapped a bandage around it and then glanced up at Fiona. "Sister, please do not tell me that you were sprinting through the castle."

"I was not."

"Then did you find a nice tree to climb instead?" Hans joked.

"Et tu, Hans?"

The reason for their remarks being so similar to those Baron Clayburn had made was that Fiona had broken her ankle as an overly spirited youth. She knew it was just affectionate teasing, but not once since she turned eighteen had Fiona thoughtlessly run around or climbed a tree or wall on a whim. Besides, she had been at the royal castle! It wasn't like a park or a playground with lots of trees.

"For how long must you torment me over something that happened when I was five and ten years old?"

"You forget, Miss Fiona, but it also happened when you were fifteen. Don't you remember what happened when Reginald was here?"

"Th-that was three years past!" The incident in question took place when her uncle returned from a trip. Fiona ran down the stairs to greet him and lost her footing.

As a grown woman, she could not endure the reminders of things she wished to be forgotten, but having broken her foot three times now, it was unsurprising that they didn't believe her about her conduct.

"Since she broke her foot at five, ten, and fifteen, that must mean that the next time it happens will be when she's twenty," Hans mused.

"So two years from now? Which means that your foot will be all better again soon."

"Enough, you two." Fiona turned away, indignant and red in the face.

Cecilia finished securing the bandage around Fiona's ankle. "There, all done. The swelling doesn't look too bad, but please do refrain from running for the time being."

"I shall."

"And no skipping or dancing either," Cecilia reminded her with a chuckle.

"I won't!"

Cecilia was born with a weak constitution, and she spent more time reading indoors than playing outside. As a result, she was rather self-possessed for her age and often seemed more mature than Fiona, despite being the younger sister.

Her hair was a glistening blonde, her eyes a much lighter amber than Fiona's. More and more, Cecilia resembled their mother, of whom Fiona had only distant memories and a lone family portrait.

Fiona stared at her sister's face for a moment, then placed a hand on her cheek. "Your complexion looks good at the moment. I'm happy you stayed up to wait for us, but it's bad for your health to be up so late. We wouldn't want you to get another fever."

"I have been feeling perfectly fine recently, so don't worry. But enough of me, I want to hear about the castle. Did anything wonderful happen while you were there?"

"Wonderful?" Immediately, memories of the incident in the garden came back to her. Feeling on the verge of blushing again, Fiona deflected. "There was a garden—a garden that people aren't typically allowed to enter. It was very pretty. There was a water fountain with an intricate design and lots of flowers in the flower bed... Oh, and I saw Norman. And Olga too."

Cecilia's eyes went round when she heard Norman's name. "How was he?"

"You just saw him during his recent visit. Naturally, he was the same. Hmm... I guess the only thing different about him was that he had new clothes?"

"Oh, Sister," Cecilia protested, but Fiona and Norman had been friends since they were young enough to run around with runny noses without caring. No matter how much older they got or how they dressed themselves up, they treated one another the same as always. Still, although they were of the same rank and distantly related, House Hayes was wealthy, unlike Fiona's family. With his good looks, gentle personality, and status as the youngest son, Norman was a hot commodity among women with families in need of a male heir. He was so popular that Fiona sometimes received thorny looks from other girls when she danced with him.

But the two of them are something else altogether.

She thought of Giles, with his astonishing, icy good looks that made him the picture of composure, and Richard, who was sociable and carried an alluring air. The pair of them were often compared to night and day, or even the moon and sun. In the past, Fiona took the comparison with a grain of salt, but having now seen the two men in person, she found she agreed with the sentiment.

It was a disrespectful comparison to make, but Giles and Richard were equals in being as handsome as the crown prince was extolled to become.

"Speaking of Norman," Fiona told her sister, "he said he would come to visit this weekend."

"Did he? I'll have to make sure we have a pie baked for him." Cecilia's expression brightened at hearing that the man she adored as an older brother would visit, so Fiona teased her.

"Hee hee. You're always so sweet on him."

"Oh?" Cecilia reddened. "I-I didn't mean to be."

"And Norman's always bringing you gifts and flowers."

"He only did that because I was ill."

While Cecilia was doing much better as of late, she was confined to her bed for some time previously.

Norman had always brought flowers that were in season and picture books for his childhood friend when she couldn't go outdoors to play. He continued this habit of his to this day. Fiona never felt envious about it; if anything, she thought it was sweet.

Cecilia grabbed the medicine box and stood, flustered. "I-I'm going to put this away and then go to bed."

"All right. Good night. Thank you for taking care of my ankle."

"Good night." She gave Fiona a hug, trying to hide her pink cheeks.

In the same moment, their father called for Hans, so both Hans and Cecilia beat a hasty retreat. Now alone, Fiona gingerly lifted her legs onto the sofa to cradle her knees.

She really does adore Norman as a brother... How is she going to react when she finds out that he's going to become her actual brother?

Fiona did like Norman, but only as a brother. It was a different kind of love than the kind her father and mother shared, and she had no doubt that Norman felt the same. If anything, Cecilia was the one who had stronger affections for him. *She's never had a chance to socialize with any other men besides him. Though, I suppose that might change soon.*

Whether or not political motives existed, it was best for a marriage to involve romantic feelings. If Norman must marry a Clayburn daughter to succeed their house, then it would not be too late to consider Cecilia as a possibility when she came of marriageable age the following year.

Fiona's father wanted her to marry Norman out of parental affection for her—he wanted to make sure his free-spirited daughter was safe and secure. Fiona was able to tell as much by how she had been raised.

Nevertheless...

It's not that I'm opposed to the very idea of marriage. It's just that I want to work and see the world. Is it so wrong to wish for an independent life?

It wasn't that she wanted to displease her family, but when she thought of the near future, Fiona felt as though the walls were closing in around her, laying a trap.

She heaved a long sigh as she looked at the perfectly wrapped bandage.

TRUE LOVE
Fades Away When the
Contract Ends

One Star in the Night Sky

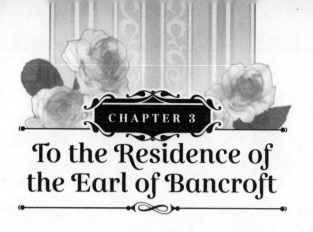

CHAPTER 3

To the Residence of the Earl of Bancroft

THE FOLLOWING AFTERNOON, Fiona found herself inside a carriage again. This time, however, she was not accompanied by her father. Across from her sat a scowling Hans, the man who had served House Clayburn for many years.

Her father and sister had urged her to rest at home until her injury was better, so she snuck out after lunch with Hans as her chaperone.

"Miss Fiona, will you truly not reconsider?"

Fiona made a frustrated sound. "I wish you would stop asking that already."

"You could easily return the object you found tomorrow or the day after." Hans didn't say it out loud, but from the pained way he looked at Fiona's foot, it was clear he thought she would be better off at home.

"It hardly hurts at all anymore thanks to the poultice. More importantly, I should return this as soon as possible. I'm sure he must be looking for it." Fiona forced a smile as she patted the reticule resting in her lap. The small, intricately embroidered handbag had been a gift from her uncle. Inside it was the cuff link that Fiona had found caught on her sleeve the night before. After checking the crest engraved on it in her almanac this morning, she discovered that it was indeed the crest of the Earl of Bancroft's house.

"I could deliver it on your behalf."

"This is the kind of thing that should be returned directly. Plus, I do not know yet whether or not this actually belongs to him."

Crests also served as a means of identification. They varied in subtle ways from individual to individual even within the same house. The crest on the cuff link had been simplified, however, so she could not identify precisely whose it was.

For an individual to have something bearing the crest of another family was proof that their families had a connection. Of course, things weren't always that straightforward, but this crest in particular was that of a very powerful noble family. By showing this, she could go shopping without a single cent on hand, or possibly even borrow money. If the possessor of the crest committed a crime or some other offense, the earl's family might be suspected of involvement. This was an item that required careful handling.

The postal service may be convenient, but it was not unheard of for packages to go missing. Postal workers had even been targeted by thieves. After taking all these possibilities into account, as the person who had found it, Fiona decided that it would be safest for her to return the cuff link to Giles personally.

"Your diligence and initiative certainly are rare virtues, but I do wish you would extend the same considerations to yourself." Hans knew that Fiona could rarely be swayed once she had made up her mind about something, but looking utterly perplexed, he tried anyway.

"All I did was twist my ankle a bit. I'm not unwell or anything."

"But perhaps you should have written a letter first requesting an appointment with him."

Fiona shrugged off his insistent appeals. "People from their house are unlikely to bother replying to every young girl with whom they have no relation whatsoever. Any letter I wrote would land in the rubbish bin before they so much as glanced at its contents. And then I would never be able to return it."

"That may be so, but then it would be their fault for ignoring you."

"Hans, please do not speak in such an unfeeling way." She knew well enough how worried he was about the condition of her foot, but Hans had always been the overprotective sort.

"It's not that I'm callous, it's that you are too kind."

"Kind? Oh, I wouldn't call it that." She was only going this far because she felt a kinship with Giles over their shared aversion to marriage. Fiona saw it more as sympathy than kindness.

Based on what she overheard yesterday, Giles's family was pressuring him to marry. Relations among them had soured because of his continual rejection of potential matches. If it were discovered that he lost an accessory with their crest on it...

Were she in Giles's position, she would be undertaking a secret, desperate search for the object.

"All will be well, Hans. So long as I show this letter of introduction from Lord Talbott, I highly doubt that even the family of an earl would refuse to receive us."

Lord Talbott was the former prime minister. They were acquainted by chance, and he had written a letter of introduction for Fiona should she ever need it.

"Yes, speaking of which! With a letter like that from Lord Talbott, you could even request an audience with the king himself. I was hoping you would save it for a time when you really needed it!"

"Goodness, an audience with the king would be far too grand for someone like me. It would be better not to have the opportunity. Which is why I think the letter is put to good use now." Fiona smiled brightly as she pointed out that the letter would likely go to waste otherwise, and Hans smiled back at her. His master's daughters they may be, but Hans had known Fiona and Cecilia since they were born. He watched them grow up and loved them both as he would his own granddaughters.

"Let's stop by the gallery after we finish dropping off the cuff link. I'm sure there must be a mountain of papers waiting for me, and perhaps Uncle has even written back."

After a pause, Hans replied, "Miss Fiona, please don't tell me that was your true goal with this outing."

"Oh dear, have you figured it out then?"

"I cannot permit you to do any work today. You are injured." He sighed as he pressed his fingers against his forehead.

"I won't work long. Just three hours!"

"No."

"Then two!"

"No."

"One and a half! Please, I beg you!"

With Fiona imploring and clinging to his arm, Hans was forced to relent. "If you must." Ultimately, he could not refuse a request from Fiona.

"Thank you, Hans! You're the best."

"But you must remember, we have an agreement: an hour and a half and not a minute more."

Fiona laughed at this emphasis on the agreed-upon timeframe just as the carriage came to a stop in front of the gates to the Earl of Bancroft's estate.

Just as Hans had warned, it was an inviolable rule that one must make an appointment before visiting a noble's home. Unexpected visits from friends were permitted, but it was a matter of course that a girl from a low-ranking house with no prior official acquaintance would be thrown out at once. However, a letter of introduction from Lord Talbott was an exceptional asset.

"You're looking for someone, you say?" The earl's butler seemed the unflappable sort, but he raised an eyebrow minutely as he fixed his gaze upon Fiona.

"That is correct. I apologize for my indiscretion in showing up unannounced, but I believe this matter warrants calling on Lord Lowell."

Based on how the women had addressed him last night, she was in fact certain that the man she was looking for now was Giles Bancroft. But because they hadn't introduced themselves in the garden, Fiona was not yet formally acquainted with him. Therefore, Fiona needed to imply that there was some doubt as to whom she needed to meet.

Noble etiquette dictated that Fiona couldn't ask to meet with Giles, heir to the earl. She could only say that she sought the owner of the lost cuff link, whom she heard asserting that he didn't wish to marry. That was why she had given the butler two letters: the first was the letter of introduction from Lord Talbott assuring her identity, while the second sought confirmation that Giles was the owner of the cuff link.

"Please follow me to the parlor, Miss Clayburn."

"That's all right. I would ask that you deliver the letter for me first. If he has no idea what I am here to return, then I do not wish to take up any more of his time."

"Very well." Hearing that, should Giles wish, Fiona would depart without insisting upon the meeting, the butler nodded with deep satisfaction. He led Fiona and Hans to a corner of the foyer before quietly ascending the stairs.

Nervous, Fiona sat on the visibly expensive sofa and whispered to Hans, who stood nearby. "Even on the inside it's extraordinarily magnificent. I can hardly believe the distance we had to go from the front gate to the front door! And this hall alone could fit the entire first floor of our town house."

The spacious entrance hall featured an enormous fireplace. The ceiling was as tall as those found in the royal palace, and from it hung a luxurious chandelier.

"This is the residence of the renowned Earl of Bancroft, after all. I hear that the principal residence in their fief is even bigger."

"It must be a dizzying sight. Oh, and they have many splendid paintings, just as I heard! Uncle would be so pleased if he were here right now!"

Multiple generations of earls had been famous for their appreciation of the artwork owned by this family. The walls were adorned with numerous masterpieces. The oil painting before her now, which depicted a scene from a myth, and many other such pieces were so monumental they could hang in the main exhibition hall of a museum. There were several sculptures in the hall as well. Fiona asked to wait here in part so that she could appreciate them at length.

Fiona was ecstatically admiring the art when she and Hans were happened upon by two maids carrying cleaning equipment. They were startled to see unexpected visitor and were about to leave the way they came when Fiona stopped them. She chatted with them until they heard footsteps coming down the same set of stairs up which the butler had gone.

"Oh, please excuse us, Miss."

"P-pardon us!"

"Thank you for speaking with me. I enjoyed our chat." Fiona watched them go with a crooked smile. It seemed almost as if they were fleeing. Unlike Fiona's household, where the few staff they had were like family to them, the Earl of Bancroft's household seemed to keep to a strict separation of master and servant.

"He is coming this way now," Hans whispered in Fiona's ear. "Oh ho, he is quite handsome. Are you sure it's him?"

"Yes, I'm pretty sure that's what he looked like," Fiona whispered back.

There was no mistaking it: the man coming down the stairs was the man Fiona had met last night. Silky, dark blond hair; long limbs that lent him an air of symmetry... Her impression last night was that he was as handsome as a work of art, and seeing him now in the light did more than simply confirm that notion.

She felt as if there was a slight shadow cast over his eyes. Perhaps he had spent the night searching for his missing cuff link. If so, she pitied him and hoped to help him obtain peace of mind at once. Fiona looked up at him on the stairs and their eyes met. His normally blank face seemed to betray a hint of surprise.

Hmm, does he remember me? Oh, I doubt it.

Giles must have spoken with countless people at last night's party. There was no way he would remember a woman he briefly met in a dimly lit garden and barely even spoke to. Fiona knew her looks were unremarkable; best to assume that, if he was surprised, it was because he didn't remember her at all.

Giles finished descending the stairs and walked over to Fiona. He was so tall, she had to look up to meet his eyes, just as she had the previous night.

"You're Miss Clayburn, I take it? I apologize for my servants' discourtesy."

"Not at all. It was I who addressed them first. Please do not find fault with them." After all, they were just passing by when she asked them to stop and chat with her. In the Clayburn household, there was frequent conversation between the family and their servants. She didn't want the maids here to get in trouble just because she behaved as she would at home.

Giles agreed to her request and then fixed his gaze upon her. She returned his searching look with a smile, then curtsied as per the etiquette that was drummed into her.

"I am Fiona Clayburn. I apologize for calling upon you so unexpectedly."

"And I am Giles Bancroft." Now that they had exchanged names, Giles invited Fiona further inside his home. "Please, follow me so that we can discuss the matter that brings you here today."

He walked away, giving Fiona, who was reaching for her reticule to give him the cuff link, no choice but to follow. She trailed after him a few steps before Giles stopped and turned around.

Huh? What's he doing? Fiona was taken aback. Panicked, she mentally reviewed her conduct up until that point, then noticed that Giles was looking at her feet.

"I hope you will excuse my asking, but are you injured?"

Fiona was startled. "Oh...yes, I twisted my ankle a little bit." She answered honestly—to attempt to conceal it would only be more conspicuous—but she hadn't expected him to actually notice. Not only was she certain she had walked normally and that he couldn't see the bandage, she was also walking behind him. Fiona glanced at Hans to find he also looked surprised. "I apologize for coming to you in such an unseemly way."

"No, that's not why I'm asking. It happened last night, didn't it?" Giles's reply left her even more surprised. Here she had been under the assumption that he didn't remember her at all.

I guess he's more observant than I thought. He has a good memory too.

He truly was meant to become earl if he had an eye for even the most trivial details. Fiona seemed to have misjudged his disposition. Giles's expression remained as rigid as ever, but she sensed something akin to regret in it. Perhaps he felt some measure of responsibility for her injury. While it was true that Fiona had been injured because of a woman's intent on Giles, that did not mean that it was his fault. If anything, Giles had saved her during that moment.

Fiona shrugged sheepishly. "It's because I am unaccustomed to wearing shoes like the ones I wore last night."

"But—"

"My little sister took it upon herself to act as the elder sister and take care of me. In fact, she rather enjoyed it." She assured him, smiling, that the swelling had gone down and she was much better now.

Giles appeared to accept this, but when they reached the bottom of the stairway, he presented his arm to Fiona. She stared for a moment, uncertain, and then felt Hans's elbow in her back.

"Miss! Your hand! He's trying to escort you!"

She looked up again at Giles, who glanced away awkwardly.

"At least allow me to offer you some support."

"Oh, thank you?"

It may have been her imagination, but she thought Giles's expression relaxed somehow at her intonation that turned her words into a question. Fiona placed her arm securely under his and took her time proceeding up the stairs. Giles brought them to a second-floor parlor.

"Wait in there," Giles instructed Hans, indicating an adjoining room. "The door is already open."

Hans gave Fiona a questioning look. Likely, Giles didn't want an outsider, even a servant, to bear witness to their conversation. Fiona nodded at Hans and gave him an assuring smile, though he was clearly worried by this turn of events. This was Giles's home. Besides, given the difference in their respective ranks, they had to obey Giles's instructions.

"Hans, if you would, please."

"Very well." Hans sounded reluctant. "Please call me if you need anything,"

Having left Hans outside, Fiona entered the parlor. Tea was already set out on the table, and the room had two occupants: the butler who had received Fiona at the door and Richard, the man who was with Giles in the palace garden. They both looked somewhat taken aback to see Giles escorting Fiona into the room.

Giles acts as though he's used to this sort of thing, but perhaps he doesn't do it often. It wouldn't be strange for Giles to be able to conduct himself perfectly according to etiquette, despite his aversion to women. This was why she hadn't removed her hand when they reached the top of the stairs.

Richard recovered quickly and walked over to them, wearing the same smile Fiona saw the previous night. "Hi, welcome. You're the one we met last night, aren't you?" His voice and demeanor both shone bright as the afternoon sunlight, a direct contrast to Giles's nightlike stillness. Perhaps this was why the two of them got along. "Is it all right if I'm here as well?"

"Yes, of course. I apologize for interrupting your afternoon. I assure you this won't take long."

After a pause, Richard said, "Oh?"

Fiona was the one who showed up without a prior appointment, after all. And if Giles was fine with it, she had no objection. But there was a look of amusement in the man's eye...

He's good-humored but cunning, she thought. She could tell from his gaze that Richard was evaluating her. Richard was known for being handsome and personable, but there was clearly more to him than that; otherwise he wouldn't be able to navigate high society as skillfully as he did.

As the daughter of a baron, Fiona ranked below them both. From the familiar way Richard spoke and acted now, compared to his comportment the previous night, it was clear that he was talented at maneuvering his way through social situations. Giles, on the other hand, remained an enigma. He had kept Fiona's hand in the crook of his arm all throughout the exchange of greetings.

Why won't he let me remove my hand yet?

Giles wasn't keeping her hand there by force, but for some reason, she couldn't slip it loose. As a result, she was forced to give a one-handed half-curtsy.

Her feet sunk into plush carpet as Giles led her to the comfortable sofa. He helped ease her to a sitting position so as to not put any weight on her sore foot, and only then did he release her. The butler served tea and then exited the room, leaving Fiona alone with Giles and Richard.

Now that she and Richard had been introduced, there was no need to take on pretentious airs or make small talk about the season. Fiona produced the cuff link, which was wrapped in a handkerchief, and placed it on the table. "I'm here to return this. It's yours, right?"

Giles picked it up, examined it on both sides, and sighed in relief. Then he reached into his jacket pocket to take out another identical cuff link and place them side by side. "As you can see, this does indeed belong to me."

Seeing the cuff links next to one another, Fiona echoed his sigh. "Good. I was a bit worried that I might have the wrong person."

In the letter she had given to the butler, Fiona had not written the particulars of what she had found because she thought there was a possibility that it belonged to someone else—a son from one of their branch families, perhaps. Holding onto an article that bore another family's crest was a heavy burden. She had been eager to return it to its owner as soon as possible.

"I've been looking for this ever since I realized I'd lost it."

"I can imagine. If only I had noticed it straight away. I apologize." She wanted to ensure he understood that she did not take it and bring it home intentionally. It was clear from how Giles and Richard looked at her that they wanted an explanation, so she gave it to them. "I discovered it caught on my sleeve in the carriage on my way home."

In her usual attire, she would have noticed it immediately. The gown she wore to the palace may have been modest compared to others, but she was dressed up complete with accessories, and with the pain in her foot, she failed to notice much else.

"From the crest I deduced that it must belong to someone in the Earl of Bancroft's family. I also thought I recalled the women in the garden calling you 'Lord Giles' last night."

"So they did."

"I considered sending it by post, but I thought it would be safest to hand it over in person. That was the reason for my sudden visit."

"And I am very grateful for it. If you had handed this to anyone else, I would have trouble on my hands." Giles thanked her politely, then frowned as he imagined what could have happened. "If you had given it to my parents or elder sister, I'm sure they would have misunderstood."

"Such as I stole it?" Fiona had thought that even Giles might think so, but he was quick to correct her assumption.

"Ah, not quite. My choice of words was poor."

At Fiona's unconvinced look, Richard offered an explanation. "What he means is that they would think you were Gil's lover."

Fiona blinked with surprise. It hadn't crossed her mind, but articles bearing a family's crest were also given as gifts to lovers. Perhaps she should have been more worried about that than about accusations of theft or misuse.

She was so estranged from the customs of courtship that she had never considered this possibility. Her friend Olga, on the other hand, would have likely jumped straight to that conclusion. Perhaps Fiona should give more consideration to the many romance novels Olga recommended.

"The thought hadn't even crossed my mind."

"Ha ha, I can see as much. See, Gil, you were worried over nothing!"

After a moment, Giles replied, "Yes, I suppose."

Oh, he's smiling! Did he find her look of surprise amusing? It was a half smile, but Richard's smile had prompted a smile from Giles all the same, the very first she had seen from him.

The man was like an ice sculpture, but seeing Giles's expression come to life like this made him appear more human. In spite of her better judgment, Fiona found the sight captivating. If those ladies from last night were present, surely, they would be screeching and swooning.

"Um, well, I have completed my errand here. I think I have explained things to an acceptable degree, so if you would excuse me." Snapping back to herself, Fiona grabbed the handkerchief off the table and put it away.

"You're going home already?" Richard sounded amazed. For some reason, even Giles looked surprised.

"I only came here to return the cuff link."

Fiona had already explained how she came to take the cuff link home with her. Her business done, she stood to leave, but Richard stopped her by pointing at the table. "Wait, at least drink your tea. Dalton even went through the trouble of making it himself for us. That's a rarity."

Dalton must have been the name of the butler. After a moment's hesitation, Fiona acquiesced. "Very well, then."

Typically, such gestures were for form's sake alone, and Fiona could not understand what reason they had to keep her here any longer. Richard was of a higher status than she, however, so she could not outright refuse him.

She sat back down on the sofa and reached for the steaming cup of tea. Enjoying its aroma, she took a sip and found its flavor refreshing and mellow. "Oh, this is good," she said, accidentally letting her opinion slip.

Richard sighed in exaggerated relief and cheerfully replied, "I'm glad to hear that it's to your liking. Dalton's hard work paid off."

"Was this made with tea leaves from Valdi?"

"You can tell?"

"It has an aroma I could never forget." Fiona's uncle once brought back this kind of tea from abroad as one of her gifts. It was bitter when steeped ordinarily, but with the correct quantity of leaves and the right temperature, it produced tea with a particular smell and mellow sweetness to it. It took Fiona many tries to figure out how to steep a satisfying cup of this tea. "I hear that Valdi is covered in steep mountains. The trees for this kind of tea can only grow at high altitudes, so it's hard to plant. I also hear that there is a great deal of labor required until the leaves can be finally harvested."

This type of tea had recently become popular even in their country, but it fetched a high price due to low stock. Only House Bancroft would serve such a valuable commodity to an unexpected visitor so casually.

"Huh, you sure know a lot about it."

"My uncle visited Valdi once, you see. He told me that the view from the mountains was magnificent."

Especially in the morning, the rising sun peeking through the opening in the clouds was so close that it could not be believed, and the sky changed colors moment to moment. After hearing that it was so beautiful that her uncle could not stop staring as he clung to the rocks of the steep slopes, Fiona dreamed of seeing it for herself someday.

She thought it made for a good anecdote for the conversation, but Richard and Giles said nothing in response; they merely stared at her. After a moment she asked, "Is something the matter?"

"Oh, sorry. It's just unusual to have such a normal conversation," Richard replied.

"What do you mean?"

"Oh, never mind. I've never thought about what the view must be like from the tea plantation before. Aren't you lucky that she was the one who wound up finding your cuff link, Gil?"

There was a pause. Finally, Gil said, "Yes."

Fiona looked at them both, even more puzzled than before. Seeing the inquisitive tilt to her head, Giles gave her a small, crooked smile.

"We'd assumed it would be the worst-case scenario, you see," Richard continued.

"Worst-case scenario?" It was true that it could be used for fraud, but that could hardly be considered a worst-case scenario.

Richard had been doing most of the talking up until now, but it was Giles who answered her question. "I was worried that someone might use this cuff link to invent groundless rumors, and I would be forced to marry them as a result."

"Oh, yes," Fiona agreed with a sigh. "Being forced into marriage would certainly constitute a tragedy."

Richard seemed surprised. "You really think that?"

"I am troubled by the same kind of predicament, actually."

"Wait, don't tell me you don't want to get married either."

They probably assumed it was a luxury of a problem for any ordinary daughter of a baron to have, but not for Fiona. Richard leaned toward her with interest; he didn't seem deterred in the least, so Fiona turned to face him and explained, "I am about to be engaged. I've been thinking about it long and hard until my head hurts to try to figure out a way to avoid it."

"Why? Do you not like the man? Is he some doddering old fool?" Richard asked, blunt in his curiosity.

Fiona couldn't help but chuckle. "No, he's someone I've known since childhood. He's a good man."

"Then I don't see the problem," Giles commented. He seemed genuinely curious as well.

And he wasn't wrong. If anything, Fiona was lucky to know the man to whom she was to be engaged, instead of being married off to some stranger's family. That was something that happened frequently. "I know that, from the outside, it must appear to be a happy arrangement."

"But you're saying it's not?" Giles stopped, seemingly embarrassed to have asked such a brazen question. "I apologize. I do not mean to pry. It's only that I have never encountered a woman like you."

But Fiona shook her head at him. It was true: there weren't many women of marriageable age who went around saying, as she did, that they had no desire to marry. Even if such women existed, they wouldn't speak about it so candidly in front of new acquaintances of the opposite sex. She had unthinkingly confided in these men only because she felt down from anguishing over this alone for so long.

"There are things I want more than marriage."

"Like what?"

"I have no desire to quit my job, for one. And I would like to travel abroad." Fiona's declaration was paired with a smile on her face, causing Giles and Richard to stare in wonder.

It was rare enough for women of the peerage to work—it was rarer still for one to claim disinterest in marriage because she wished to keep working.

Even Richard, who found the whole conversation fascinating, was so surprised by this response that he asked her for confirmation. "You mean to say that you work?"

"Yes. Not officially, of course. My uncle sends paintings from all over the world, and I assist him with the work."

"Oh, so he's an art dealer?"

"Of a sort. My uncle rarely comes home, so in his place, I take care of the transportation or help negotiate with clients and art galleries. I also handle his accounts; those sorts of things."

In other words, she did all the clerical work. Her uncle wasn't good at that type of work, nor did he excel at negotiating. Fiona could not stand idly by after hearing that a painting was lost during transport, resulting in a wrongful accusation against her uncle. He nearly had to give all the money back. While she helped him out, he wound up entrusting that whole part of the business to her.

Currently, she acted as the point of contact for his gallery in the capital. When she was home at their fief, she exchanged letters with clients, and during the social season she worked at the store's office in the capital. There were times when negotiations soured and the owner needed to show his face, but for the most part, Fiona ran things behind the scenes. She may have been her uncle's representative, but her age and sex were disadvantages when it came to publicly handling such expensive commodities.

Giles and Richard exchanged a look after hearing Fiona's explanation. They probably thought her strange, but she didn't care whether these people judged her. She thought it unlikely that she would speak with them ever again.

More importantly, she felt lighter now, having unburdened herself of the thoughts she had kept bottled up. *I probably shouldn't have told them all that, but it's not like they have any connections to my house. I doubt we'll ever meet again, so who cares?*

Fiona expected them to be exasperated by her confession. Instead, Giles murmured in admiration, "It sounds like you're working as a secretary."

"Does it? I've never thought of my work as being similar to such a difficult position."

It wasn't like her uncle sent her new paintings that frequently, after all. What she did was an assortment of routine tasks, nothing particularly stressful.

Working had helped her make some personal connections in the world. She felt like she barely made any money, but she enjoyed getting to handle objects of beauty. She equally enjoyed the opportunity to speak with and get to know all sorts of people, regardless of their rank.

She summarized these thoughts, which seemed to only provide more food for thought, and Giles and Richard encouraged her to keep talking, with airs of great interest.

"So, when you say you wish to live abroad, you mean with your uncle?" Richard asked.

"That's right. It seems much more efficient to accompany him, you see. I would also like to search for ways to help my family's fief.

The Clayburn family isn't known for anything in particular. At any rate, seeing the world has been a dream of mine since I was small, and that's my biggest motivation." She revealed that she had planned to leave the following year, once her sister came of age. "I've even been studying foreign languages for this purpose. But if I get married, then I won't be able to keep working *or* be away from home, now, will I?"

"That is indeed how it would go, ordinarily. So, your family arranged your betrothal without your consent?"

"My father planned it in secret, hoping to settle down his overly spirited daughter. I'm not sure if it's a good thing or not that I found out." Fiona sighed and rested her cheek in her hand. She knew perfectly well that preventing her betrothal would mean disobeying her father, but Fiona could not so easily give up on the dream she had cherished since she was young. "It feels like he's about to finish building the moat to keep me trapped in his castle... Oh, my apologies. Here I've been rambling on about myself this whole time."

"No apology necessary. Your situation is quite intriguing. Allow me to take the opportunity to ask: Have you no desire to marry, whomever it may be?"

"Well, I'd at least like it put it off for a few years."

"I see. In that case, what if Gil or myself asked for your hand in marriage?"

"Wait," Giles interjected, leaning toward Richard in confusion. "What are you saying, Rick?" Fiona stared in shock, wondering the same thing.

Richard had a scheming smile upon his face as he assured his friend he was just joking. Realizing that this was just Richard's way of teasing his friend, Fiona began to laugh. "As if that would ever be possible! But I would reject you both all the same."

"Ha ha ha! Such a quick rejection too. Yes, I think I've just hit upon a brilliant idea." Richard clapped his hands and winked at the two of them. "You two should court."

TRUE
LOVE
Fades Away
When the
Contract
Ends

One Star in
the Night Sky

CHAPTER 4

Her One and Only Chance

RICHARD HELD A FINGER UP. Fiona fixed her gaze upon it as she took in Richard's words: "You two should court."

Lord Lowell and me? Court?

Having processed the suggestion, she and Giles asked in unison, "What?"

Against her better judgment, Fiona turned to look at Giles. He returned her wide-eyed look with one of his own. His handsome, grayish-blue eyes, normally so cold and unfeeling, looked surprisingly pretty in this display of emotion.

Richard laughed. "See, you're already working in tandem!"

"Wait, what?"

"You two should have no trouble pretending to be in love."

"Pretending to be in love?" Again, Giles and Fiona spoke in unison, which made Richard laugh even harder.

Giles stood and advanced on Richard. Fiona scrambled to get her thoughts in order. "Now, hold on a minute. Why would you even suggest such a thing?"

"Hear me out. Miss Clayburn, I'm sure that you could tell after everything that happened last night, but Gil is also having troubles that relate to dealings with the opposite sex."

Giles's aversion to women was common knowledge. So was his rejection of any hint of marriage that came his way. There was no point in denying it, so Fiona merely nodded. "Um, yes, I could."

"Gil has zero interest in marriage, yet every time he attends a party, he's chased around like he was last night. He's always forced to run and hide from other attendees who want to speak to him."

That certainly sounded bothersome. Yet Giles had to attend such functions regardless; high society could be so aggravating. Fiona frowned. "That sounds awful."

"Indeed. However, Gil doesn't have a good reason to be so opposed to marriage, unlike yourself."

"You are being extraordinarily rude, Rick."

"He doesn't need a good reason, if you ask me." Fiona's objection earned her yet another surprised look from Giles and another smile from Richard. She continued seriously, "I think not wanting it is reason enough. Especially because I can sense in my heart that it's how you truly feel. I feel it myself: it's an uncanny sensation, like being wrapped in darkness."

Not knowing why but feeling scared, not knowing why but finding the notion disagreeable—each of these were respectable reasons to not want to marry.

"If only he could explain with a concrete example, then I'm sure others would also understand."

In the wake of this declaration from Fiona, Giles's fury at Richard vanished. After a moment he admitted, "That's an interesting way to put it."

"I just believe that if we were able to express in words everything that we feel in our hearts, then we would have no need for paintings or songs." Whenever Fiona felt she couldn't get her feelings in order about something, she found that paintings and music could help. It was experiencing that firsthand that made her so devoted to helping her uncle with his work. Fiona looked back up at Richard. "Oh, I'm sorry. We've gone off topic."

Richard cleared his throat and nodded. "Ah, no, that's all right. To summarize, though: you wish to avoid becoming engaged in the near future, and Gil wants to keep all his admirers at bay. I thought it would only made sense for the two of you to pretend to be a couple."

It could work as a diversion, having someone pretend to fill that role. It wouldn't outright put a stop to the hopeful young ladies seeking Giles's hand, but Richard seemed proud of his idea and confident that it would provide Giles with a suitable excuse for rejecting his pursuers.

"I apologize for my impoliteness in asking, but I presume that this friend to whom you are to be engaged to is of lower status than Giles?"

"That is correct. He is of the same status as me—from the house of a baron."

"Then that makes things easier. Your family would be hard-pressed to deny Gil."

The difference in social rank held enormous sway. It was hard to imagine a circumstance under which someone would attempt to defy the heir of so powerful a house as Giles's. The plan was beginning to seem more realistic to Fiona, but Giles said sullenly, "Rick, can't you come up with a less ridiculous-sounding solution?"

"What solution would that be? I think this plan is the best way to solve both of your problems."

"I mean, she and I only just met."

"All the better, if you ask me. Since you've only just met, you can say that fate brought you together and you fell in love at first sight. That should quell any objections."

Richard's confidence in this proposal made Giles heave a great, exasperated sigh. But Fiona, for her part, was seriously considering the idea.

He's right—if I had someone I loved, then...

Her father had yet to inform her of her betrothal to Norman, so she could hardly be blamed for having found herself a man. And her parents were unusual for nobles in that they married for love. Her father still loved his late wife dearly, so Fiona was confident that he wouldn't force the matter with Norman if she found a love match. And even if he did object—

"At the very least, this should buy me some time." Her father planned to announce her betrothal to Norman at a party being held at their home. As the Clayburns weren't wealthy, they did not often hold balls at their own residence—once per season, twice at most. So her first task was to survive the party in half a month's time. If they kept up the charade for a whole year, then by the time the next season came around, Cecilia would be an adult, and Fiona could go and travel with her uncle.

"Miss Clayburn?"

Fiona was so absorbed in figuring out how Richard's proposed plan would work that she hadn't even heard Giles, still visibly confused, trying to address her. Holding her cheeks in her hands, she said, "Oh my. After giving the idea due consideration, I believe it to be a wonderful proposal."

"See?" said Richard, satisfied to hear Fiona taking his idea seriously.

Giles, however, pressed a hand to his forehead, evidently unconvinced. "Wait, you two. Let's not get ahead of ourselves."

"Listen, Gil, I'm about at my limit for having to save you during every single ball."

"And I do feel sorry for that."

Richard was sociable, the kind to enjoy parties, so he probably wished he could spend more time enjoying them. Based on his humble apology, Giles must have felt indebted to him.

"Besides," Richard continued, "this weekend's soirée is at the Earl of Burleigh's residence, isn't it? Lady Caroline must be lying in wait to sink her claws into you."

"Ugh..."

"Wouldn't it be nice to only have to dance with her just the once?"

For Fiona's benefit, Richard explained that Lady Caroline was the ringleader of the young ladies who chased after them in the garden the night before. Out of all those women, she certainly did seem to be the most taken with Giles.

But of course, Giles couldn't run away from the host of a party. He sunk into silence with a sour expression on his face. Fiona asked, "My apologies, Lord Lowell, but do you receive many offers from potential matches even when you return to your fief after the season's end?"

"What's that?"

"Do women pursue you all the way to your fief?"

"No, they don't go to such extreme lengths. Why do you ask?"

"Then why don't we see how it goes at this ball this weekend? If the charade seems effective, then we can continue it." There was no guarantee that Richard's plan would work, but they wouldn't know unless they tried. The two of them were at the end of the line, with no other solution available. "Let's give it half a month at least, until the end of the season at most, while we're both still in the capital."

So long as she could postpone the announcement of her engagement, Fiona would be satisfied. And she was certain that Giles wanted a way to deflect the fierce attacks of other young women while he was in the capital.

Fiona straightened her posture and looked Giles in the eye. She had to make what she said next clear for his sake, given his discomfort with women's advances and distaste for the idea of marriage. "Don't worry. I won't deviate from our charade. I swear to you that I shan't fall in love with you."

Richard burst out laughing. "She's actually swearing it," he said, but Fiona looked completely serious.

"If you're worried, then I'm happy to take an oath or sign a contract. I shall not develop any romantic affections for you."

"Miss Clayburn—"

"Appreciation of the arts is my job and my hobby. I adore beautiful things, but on the other hand, I'm used to seeing them. I am not the type to fall head over heels because of someone's good looks."

Richard laughed louder than ever at Fiona's solemn words. Giles looked even more bewildered than before. "Brilliant! Gil, she's completely immune to your looks."

"I think he is quite handsome. However, that has no effect on me when it comes to romance."

"Then what about me?"

"Why, Lord Russel, you're handsome in a different way. I apologize, but I do not wish to elaborate."

"Ha ha ha ha! That's fine. I love it." Richard was holding his sides with laughter, as if Fiona's assessment were the funniest thing in the world. A smile even tugged at Giles's lips. Fiona was pleased to see that he could find humor in the conversation, despite its topic.

But of course. Even if he's known as the Icy Scion, he's still a man—of course he feels emotions.

The changes in his countenance were rare, but whenever they happened, she got a glimpse into the inner workings of his heart through his grayish-blue eyes. Fiona realized then that even she had been caught up in her preconceptions about him based on the rumors she had heard.

And that was all they were—preconceptions.

When she put them aside and considered the situation, Richard's suggestion was outrageous but likely her only chance.

She had never heard of people pretending to be lovers except in novels or plays. The very fact that such schemes were so unrealistic meant that people were unlikely to be suspicious.

"I mean, I really am out of options," Fiona said. "Don't you feel the same, Lord Lowell?"

"I admit I am fed up with the situation, but I remain unconvinced that this plan would work."

"Really? I have a feeling that those who love gossip will happily take the bait. I may not be a good match for you, but that could actually work in our favor—it might add to the plan's credibility."

"I wouldn't say that you're not a good match," Richard put in. But Fiona thought it was obvious to see when she and Giles stood next to one another. Everyone was sure to come up with humorous rumors about them, and probably not the kind that Fiona would find pleasing.

Privately, Fiona knew that she shouldn't be stubborn—that she should just accept her engagement to Norman quietly, but her heart wouldn't stop whispering that she shouldn't just accept it.

Once a person was engaged, it was difficult to break that engagement. If she said she wanted to break off her engagement to someone with whom there was no fault, it would create a fissure between their families, who up until now had enjoyed amiable relations. This was her one and only chance to prevent it before it happened.

"If there's no other option, then I'll just have to run away from home," Fiona murmured, dropping her gaze.

Giles and Richard both gasped. They hadn't expected her to consider such drastic measures.

"Otherwise, the only other choice I would have would be death. Running away would be preferable."

"That's rather extreme."

"Then do you have any other ideas for how I could peacefully make sure this engagement never happens?"

"No... I suppose not," Giles agreed reluctantly.

"Then there you have it. Moreover, I'm pretty sure that not having to marry me would be better for him as well."

She could not picture herself as the one standing at the altar with Norman. She could only picture Cecilia wearing the veil at his wedding. *Whether that happens will be up to them. All I know is that I should not be the one by his side.*

She grew up playing with Norman and cared dearly for him. He could be a bit unreliable at times, but no one was perfect. That was exactly why Fiona wanted him to marry someone out of love, not obligation.

Her father did his best to make up for their mother's absence by doting on her. And of course, she loved Cecilia very much. She didn't want to have to leave Hans and the other servants either.

"I loathe the idea of hurting my family by running away. If there were any other option, I would take it, no matter what it was."

"Do you truly mean it?"

"Yes, from the bottom of my heart. Please, Lord Lowell, won't you help me?"

For a short moment, Fiona and Giles gazed into one another's eyes. But just as Giles was about to speak, the door flew open with a bang and a stunningly beautiful woman burst into the room in a flurry of skirts.

This woman who had made such a grand entrance looked just like Giles. "So this is where you've been. I've been searching everywhere for you!"

"Sister?"

Behind the woman stood a man who looked like a clerk; he carried with him something rectangular that was wrapped in a sheet. A tall man, who must have been his employer, followed the clerk into the room.

The door had been left wide-open, and just outside of it they could see Dalton the butler pressing his fingers to his brow, as well as a wide-eyed Hans.

Sister? Oh, she must be the Marchioness of Colet!

Lady Miranda Colet, to be exact—daughter of the Earl of Bancroft and Giles's biological older sister. The royal family had attended her wedding at the cathedral; it had been the talk of the capital. She was known for her beauty and for being the soul of social gatherings, even after becoming marchioness.

As the daughter of a baron, Fiona had little contact with people from the families of earls or marquises. They even attended different kinds of parties, so she had never seen the Marchioness before. She had, however heard a lot from her friend Olga.

She really is as beautiful as they say.

While Giles looked like a sculpture, his sister Miranda looked like a goddess from a painting. She had the same dark blonde hair and grayish-blue eyes as her brother, but she was even more radiant than he, likely because of the air with which she carried herself. She looked lovely in her dress, which was the color of the summer sky, and every accessory she so casually wore was exquisite.

"I'm glad you're here too, Rick. I would like you to take a look at this painting... Oh, is this a friend of yours, Rick?"

"Oh, I'm—" Fiona stood up to introduce herself, but Miranda took one look at her and continued prattling on with excitement.

"That's all right. You may look upon it as well!"

Giles sighed with resignation. Richard shrugged and gave Fiona a look, from which Fiona deduced that Miranda was always like this. She gave him a small nod back.

The reason Miranda was so excited and pushy was likely that she felt relaxed in her family home. Both the Earl of Bancroft and the Marquis of Colet had residences in great locations here in the capital. Fiona was surprised by her sudden entrance, but it wasn't strange for Miranda to frequently visit her home.

The clerk carrying the package reverently removed the cloth to reveal what was underneath. Miranda put her hands on her hips, puffed up with pride. "This is Raymond's newest work!"

It was a beautiful painting of a small bird. The bird's wings and back were brown, the down on its belly white, and it had red on its forehead and breast. It sat on a branch, in a forest in early winter.

It was in a big frame, but the painting itself was on the smaller side—the size of a dinner tray. It would be easy to hang most anywhere.

"Well, well," said Richard, "it's a common redpoll. By Raymond, do you mean Raymond Bailey? You've been wanting one of his paintings for a while, haven't you?"

Miranda nodded, gazing with obvious delight at the painting. "That's right, Rick. And now I finally have one. What do you think? Isn't it lovely?"

Raymond Bailey was a modern painter who was enjoying a bout of popularity. His work—detailed paintings of small animals and landscape paintings with an exotic mood—were in the highest demand. However, he never painted the same kind of piece twice, so he had few works. He also only worked with one select dealer, making it nearly impossible to procure his art.

"Did you buy this, Sister?"

"I'm just about to. I had it brought here because I wanted you and Mother to have a look first."

The painter himself never made public appearances, nor did he accept commissions. No one could even say whether Raymond Bailey was his real name. He concealed the details of his private life, so his identity was shrouded in mystery. Not only was he popular, but he was also possessed of true skill: even the palace had his work hanging in its private spaces.

"This is Mr. Gordon. He has just opened a new gallery on Low Street. He said he has connections to people who know Raymond, and so he managed to procure Raymond's newest work for me before it has even been publicly announced!"

"That is correct," said the brown-haired man Miranda had just introduced, stroking his well-groomed mustache. "I procured this for Lady Colet." He treated the room to an overly reverent bow.

Gordan appeared to be a little younger than Fiona's father. He had a deep voice and something of a shadow cast over his long eyes. He must have been quite attractive in his youth; he seemed more fit to be an actor than an art dealer.

He placed a hand confidently on the frame, explaining, "This may be a small painting, but you can fully admire the charm of Raymond's style in it."

"It's truly lovely. Don't you agree, Rick?" Miranda sought Richard's approval instead of her brother's, who showed very little interest in the affair.

"I do think it's pretty and all, but paintings are beyond my purview."

"Oh, you."

"This is one of Raymond's works?" Fiona murmured. "And you claim it's a new one that hasn't been unveiled to the public yet?" She had been staring intently at the painting since the cloth had been removed.

Giles was standing right next to her, so he heard her. "Miss Clayburn?"

Fiona continued talking to herself, oblivious to all else but the painting. "The bird is charming. It's a painting of the highest quality."

"Just so. Even young women such as yourself know the charm of Raymond's works." With a quick, calculating gaze, Gordon took in Fiona's modest dress as he gave this pompous response.

"While it is indeed a beautiful painting, unfortunately, this is not one of Raymond's works," Fiona declared, so decisive and assertive that everyone stared at her in amazement. All the while, she did not take her eyes off the painting. "It uses the colors he prefers, and the composition and finishing touches are quite similar. It's a very convincing fake."

Gordon's eyebrows rose. "I cannot ignore such an accusation. However, I can only assume that someone like you has never before had the opportunity to lay your eyes upon one of Master Raymond's works." He wore an unconcealed look of displeasure.

Fiona, however, showed no sign of backing down. If anything, Giles thought that she took on a more defiant stance—she seemed *angry*.

"It's quite easy to pick out. The shading and the softness of the bird's plumage do not demonstrate the techniques Raymond would use to express them. And the paints used for the red on the forehead and breast, as is characteristic of a common redpoll— were they also painted using Wistery paints?"

"I beg your pardon?"

"I believe Raymond prefers to use only painting supplies made by the Wistery Company, but this artist used paints from other manufacturers as well. The red is a clear example. This painting is a fake." Heedless of Gordon's scowl, Fiona continued her verbal assault. "They also did their best to mimic Master Raymond's

signature, but the angle of the 'y' is incorrect. I must reiterate: this is a very good imitation. It wouldn't surprise me if a professional art dealer determined it to be real."

"You have some nerve, Miss." Incensed, Gordon's voice took on a threatening tone as he stepped toward her.

Giles reached out an arm to protect her, but Fiona ignored him and took a step of her own closer to the man, a slight smile upon her lips. Just outside the door to the room, the Earl's butler watched the scene play out with a stern look on his face. Hans, for his part, looked thoroughly exhausted by Fiona's penchant for picking fights.

"It is in bad character for a young woman to speak such nonsense. I shall take you to court."

"Go ahead. If you still do not believe me, then I have one more piece of evidence. You must know that Raymond never paints the same subject twice."

"Of course I know that." Gordon stared daggers at her. "He's never painted this kind of bird—"

"But he has painted a common redpoll before," Fiona said, delivering her coup de grace.

"What—?"

"He painted it over a decade ago; his relatives are in possession of the piece now. It was never put on the market, however, so there is no public record of it."

"H-how would you know such a thing?"

Fiona ignored Gordon's question and instead turned to offer Miranda a deep curtsy. "Please excuse my intrusion into your affairs, Lady Colet. However, Lord Lister, the head examiner of the Royal Art Academy, can verify what I have just said."

Now, not only Gordon but also Richard and Giles were astonished by Fiona's declaration. Miranda met Fiona's gaze as she crossed her willowy arms and touched her index finger to her shapely lips. "You truly believe this to be a fake?"

"There is no doubt that it was painted with exceptional skill. If you wish to possess it, then it is sure to bring you delight to look upon. However, if you ask whether this is Raymond's work, then I am obliged to say no."

"Hmm." Miranda's gaze turned cold as she fixed her jewel-like eyes upon Gordon. He had tried to use his expertise as an art dealer as a shield, but once Fiona brought up the name of the academy's head examiner—a name that no ordinary person would know—Gordon was left speechless.

Fiona offered him a way out. "I am sure that Mr. Gordon must have been deceived by someone. As I said, it does look a great deal like something Raymond would paint."

"Yes, let us leave it at that." Miranda sighed and looked around at everyone present. She produced a folding fan from somewhere and began to fan herself. "And let us have this painting properly appraised."

There was no way she would buy a painting suspected of being a fake. Hearing Miranda's words, Fiona smiled at her with relief.

"Mr. Gordon, please come back with a certificate from the academy. Once you have that, I shall be glad to pay your original asking price."

"V-very well, my lady."

"Dalton! See our guest out."

Gordon continued to glare at Fiona even as the butler escorted him and his employee out of the parlor. After they were gone, Miranda turned her attention to Fiona once again. "So, who are you, exactly?"

"Please excuse me for the delayed introduction. I am Baron Clayburn's daughter, Fiona."

"I see. And how is it that you know so much about paintings?"

"Sister, she's—"

"Sorry to interrupt, but it just so happens that I am on familiar terms with Gallery Roche on Bay Street," Fiona explained with a curtsy and a smile, stopping Giles from answering the question.

Gallery Roche was the art gallery at which Fiona worked as her uncle's point of contact. While the gallery was more recently established than some and didn't handle many paintings, its work was recognized as high quality and the gallery trustworthy to do business with. It had even purveyed paintings to the royal palace.

Miranda's expression brightened at the gallery's name. "Why, that's the only art gallery that you can buy Raymond's paintings at!"

"Since the beginning of the season, the owner has received no word from Raymond of any new works. I do not believe he would choose to deal his paintings through anyone but Roche. So while I do not mean to be rude..."

In fact, the gallery owner had recently grumbled jokingly that he wished Raymond would finish a new painting soon. Raymond was an introvert who also suffered from wanderlust. Fiona didn't know any gallery but Mr. Roche's who could keep a grip on his reins. It was impossible, then, that one of Raymond's new paintings would appear on the market elsewhere.

Still, Fiona apologized again for butting into Lady Miranda's affairs when she recognized the painting as a fake.

"That's all right. Now that you mention it, it does seem suspicious that Mr. Gordon managed to procure the painting so suddenly, and that he was rushing me to buy it."

"You can be so imprudent, Sister."

"Normally I would have looked into it. I was just anxious because I'm dying to have one of Raymond's paintings. Ah, I'm so disappointed." Miranda sat down on the sofa, then pointed her fan at Richard. "She's not your usual type. Have you had a change of heart as to the kind of women you're interested in?"

"Oh, about that—"

But Miranda had already made up her mind. "She is modest in her appearance, but even I can tell she has a good head on her shoulders. Oh, yes, Gil, there's a young woman I am dying for you to meet. Tomorrow during the Earl of Sandiana's—"

"You are mistaken, Sister," Giles interrupted, wrapping an arm around Fiona's shoulder.

Oh? Fiona looked up at him in surprise and found that his handsome face was awfully close to hers. Giles' grayish-blue eyes gazed back at her, and a fearless smile spread across his lips.

He was just so beautiful that it left her speechless.

"Miss Fiona Clayburn is *my* sweetheart."

Miranda froze, her swaying fan coming to a standstill. "What did you just say?"

"I said that she's not Richard's girlfriend—she's mine."

"S-since when? How long have you been courting? Rick, did you know about this?!"

"Please calm yourself, my lady."

"Don't you dare tell me to calm myself after hearing news like this! *Mother!*" Miranda shot to her feet, brushing Richard aside as she ran out of the room.

Giles, who still had his arm around Fiona, pressed his lips together to hold back laughter.

Oh, he's actually... Fiona had assumed that he was the conservative, buttoned-up type with no sense of humor, but it seemed she was mistaken.

When he addressed her next, Giles's mirthful expression gave way to a weary one. "Well..."

Fiona blinked. "Yes?" It seemed she was witnessing yet another side of him that she hadn't known existed.

"Well, there you have it then, Miss—no, just Fiona now." He leaned in even closer, making Fiona pull away reflexively.

"Um, I beg your pardon?" *Why are you getting so close to me?*

From the corner of her eye, she saw Richard's shoulders quivering with suppressed laughter. Just as Fiona grew a tad irritated at the men's amusement, a low and gravelly voice said, "Miss Fiona."

Fiona hadn't even noticed that Hans was now standing calmly next to them. "Oh, Hans!"

"I believe I just heard this gentleman claim to be your beau. Gracious me, I think my hearing is beginning to go."

"Ah—yes. I heard the same."

"Oh? So that is indeed what he said. Would you, perhaps, care to explain?" Hans's smile had an unusual energy about it as he stared fixedly at Giles.

Fiona was caught in the middle of their staring match. She slipped out of Giles's grasp and took Hans's hand into hers. "Um, it's a rather long story."

"That's all right with me. I would hear it from beginning to end." Now it felt as if Hans was closing in on her.

Fiona was trying to pacify him with a forced smile when Richard started clapping. "Mind if I interrupt? I would suggest you take your leave before Miranda comes back with their mother."

"He's right. Rick, buy me some time."

"You owe me," Richard said with a merry wink. "Don't forget to make date plans!"

Without so much as a chance to say goodbye, Giles took Fiona's hand and led her from the room.

They hurried through the long corridor and down the stairs. Fiona had the vague sense that Giles, having remembered her injury, lifted her into his arms and carried her the rest of the way. The next thing she knew, she was inside of the carriage.

Huh? When did I get here?

It was the baron's carriage in which she and Hans had ridden on their way over. She recognized the interior, but there was someone she was not used to seeing sitting opposite of her: Giles, with his handsome face, long legs, and crossed arms.

She wasn't sure how Giles had persuaded him, but Hans was sitting with the driver; Giles and Fiona were alone inside the carriage. Fiona looked out the window, panicked, to see that they were heading into the city center. "Where are we going?"

"Bay Street," Giles replied, as if it were the most natural thing in the world. "I heard that you were planning to go to the gallery after speaking with me."

Fiona was relieved to hear that Hans had upheld their agreement. With how angry he looked after all the commotion in the earl's residence, she wouldn't have been surprised to find that he was taking her straight home.

Giles seemed to be able to sense Fiona's relief. He turned to look at where Hans sat on the driver's bench. "I bought us some time until we arrive so that we have an opportunity to speak alone. He's a good, loyal servant."

"Hans was originally my mother's servant. He served her since she was a child. But because of that, he can be a bit overprotective at times."

"I think that's a fine quality," Giles said, averting his gaze as if lost in a memory.

Fiona hesitated, uncertain what to say next, but Giles

changed the subject. "I've decided to go along with Rick's plan. You haven't changed your mind from earlier, correct?"

So she had not misheard his declaration after all. Giles's expression was serious, so Fiona straightened her posture and adopted a similar pose. "That is correct. Thank you very much."

They were courting, but it was only going to be an act. Fiona assured him once more that she would not mistake the situation or cause him any trouble.

Giles nodded slightly and sighed. "At first, I thought it was a ridiculous idea—well, I still think it is—but sometimes you need to make small sacrifices to solve a problem."

His countenance had completely changed when Miranda expressed hopes of setting him up with a lady she knew. He was probably counting on this plan to help him avoid yet another marriage proposition. Be that as it may...

"Um, I apologize about the...commotion I caused earlier."

Fiona didn't regret preventing Lady Miranda from being swindled. Thinking back, however, she thought she could have conducted herself in a better manner; she hadn't behaved at all like a proper lady. This was the sort of thing that had motivated her father, who worried about how she could be at times, to try to marry her off. Once married, she would be confined to the house and forced to settle down.

"That's all right," Giles reassured her, his gaze softening. "Determining the authenticity of a painting is beyond my purview, but from what I could see, you were not wrong."

In truth, the change in his demeanor was minor, but it felt to Fiona as if the sheet of ice in which he kept himself protected had melted away, leaving him somewhat vulnerable. The impression bewildered her.

"My sister is the type to lose her head and forget all else when she's excited about something. I'm glad you stopped her for me."

"I-I'm glad that I could help, in that case."

Fiona knew that the manner in which she had spoken to Gordon was unbecoming of a young lady. The fact that Giles wasn't appalled by her after witnessing that behavior—and moreover, that he agreed to the plan to pretend to be in love, despite his previous refusal made Fiona think that he had strange tastes, or perhaps nerves of steel.

Perhaps seeing that made him believe that I really do have no interest in romance. That would explain his change of heart.

While Fiona was lost in her thoughts, Giles changed the topic. "We don't have much time left. For now, let's share what information we'll absolutely need to know about each other."

With the steady click-clack of the carriage filling the air around them, they fully introduced themselves to one another: their names, ages, family structures, and a brief explanation of their personal histories. They shared their hobbies too, and what they liked to do in their spare time. In no time at all, Giles covered everything that a couple would undoubtedly know about one another.

"Lord Lowell, may I—"

"I think you should stop addressing me so."

"Then shall I refer to you as Lord Giles instead?"

"You should stop speaking to me so formally," he said, but this was a difficult change for Fiona to make so abruptly.

Meanwhile, Giles began speaking to her in the same curt manner that she had heard him use with Richard in the palace garden. Though he would one day be earl, he had a lot of bothersome things to deal with, and the rules of socializing were complicated. The flexibility to quickly switch between modes of conversation was likely a necessary asset.

"It's best if we don't make this overly complicated. We'll use as much of the truth as we can."

"Meaning that we should say we first met last night at the party for the prince?"

"That's fine. Since we haven't known each other long, we can plead ignorance when asked something about one another that we genuinely don't know."

"I agree." Mixing in the truth was how you made it so that your lie wasn't discovered immediately. Fiona had heard of this method but never thought she'd find herself in a position to employ it. She felt guilty, but Giles was right—sacrifices had to be made.

"Do you think you'll have time to meet with me tomorrow?"

"Yes."

"Good. We'll hammer out the details then, including our plans from here... Oh, we've arrived."

The carriage rolled to a stop in front of the gallery and Giles exited of his own accord, without waiting for instruction.

Fiona found herself surprised by how nimble he was, then realized he was holding his hand out to her.

She froze, unsure of what he was doing. "Huh?"

"Would you rather I carry you out in my arms?"

"Th-that's all right!" Panicked, she placed her hand in his, and he carefully helped her out of the carriage. Her foot didn't even have time to hurt.

For someone who had never had a sweetheart before, he sure knew how to behave. "Um, have you really never courted a woman before?" she asked, suddenly suspicious.

Giles harumphed, a pensive look on his face. "I haven't. I was just trying to imitate Rick."

Oh! That makes sense! Richard was an expert in romance, to put it mildly; an authority on it. As she had sensed from his conduct toward her in the palace garden, Richard possessed a disposition that charmed everyone. He must be even more sweet toward his lovers.

She understood Giles's rationale. However, she thought it perhaps a bit excessive for the Icy Scion to use his lady-killer of a best friend as a model of behavior.

Before she could tell him as much, Hans came down from the driver's seat. "If you would please excuse us, Lord Giles."

"Right. I'll see you tomorrow." Giles leaned down to whisper that he would come to get her, and something brushed her cheek. By the time she realized it had been his lips, he was already climbing into his carriage, which had followed theirs from his residence.

She touched her cheek, which was beginning to feel hot, staring dumbfounded at the retreating carriage. *Don't you think you're taking this a bit far?!*

She was glad that no one had walked by and seen them. Who knew what kind of rumor would crop up if they were spotted?

Oh, wait, Fiona thought then, *maybe it would be better for people to start gossiping about us. Huh.* There would be no point to this whole charade if it wasn't widely known that they were in love. In truth, she shouldn't mind the idea of people talking about them—she should welcome it. But Fiona was still a novice when it came to romance; she didn't know the correct things to do.

I guess I'd better start reading those romance books Olga lent me when I get home. While she came to that conclusion in the span of only a few seconds, she was beginning to feel an ominous energy behind her, like something that could make the very earth quake.

"Miss Fiona."

Fiona turned around to find her family's loyal manservant wearing a look of displeasure. "Um, Hans—"

"I think we should have a little chat before you begin your work."

"Y-yes, of course. Anything you'd like." She nodded several times, then all but sprinted to open the gallery doors.

TRUE LOVE

Fades Away When the

Contract Ends

One Star in
the Night Sky

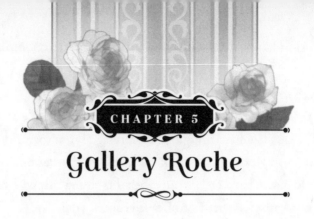

CHAPTER 5

Gallery Roche

FIONA GREETED THE EMPLOYEE working in the front, then made her way to the back office, closing the door with a decisive click. There was a letter waiting in her mailbox, but before she could attend to it, she owed Hans an explanation.

They sat together on the office's smallish sofa, and she shared a version of what had transpired between her and Giles.

"I see. So you chatted, and the two of you hit it off after you returned the cuff link."

"That's right."

"I did hear plenty of laughter coming from the room. Until that art dealer arrived, that is."

That had been Richard's laughter, but Fiona decided not to correct him.

All Hans had witnessed was Fiona cornering Gordon over the matter of the counterfeit painting. If that was all there was to the tale, then of course Hans would see no basis for romance to have blossomed. His attitude softened, however, when Fiona told him of the accident in the garden the night before.

"Oh my! So that's how you got hurt."

"You didn't think I had really gone and climbed a tree, did you?" Fiona laughed, bringing her bandaged foot forward.

Still frowning, Hans took on a less confrontational stance. "I would like to have a few words with this young lady who pushed you, but I am glad that Lord Lowell caught you."

"Me too. Without him, I would have fallen straight to the ground."

"If you had, then I would not be able to stay silent. However..." Hans sunk into thought. It seemed that something bothered him.

Fiona lowered her gaze, racked with guilt at having told even these necessary lies to Hans, who thought of her as a granddaughter. But what if someone were to find them out? The thought of Hans being blamed or rebuked for being complicit in their scheme was intolerable.

"Are you mad at me, Hans?"

"Of course not, Miss Fiona."

"But you only call me Miss Fiona when you're very angry."

"I'm not angry. I'm...worried. Your mother was around your age when she fell head over heels for your father."

Hearing this, Fiona lifted her head back up. Hans had originally been her mother's servant. He was used to caring for her, so he came with her to the Clayburn home when she married.

Hans laughed awkwardly and gazed past Fiona and out the window behind her, as if lost in a memory.

Fiona's mother had always had a weak constitution. After she met Fiona's father by chance at a resort and fell in love at first sight, she pushed through everyone's objections and married him. Then, desiring children, she pushed herself even further, resulting in her untimely demise. Fiona wished that she could have had more time with her mother, but she figured that her mother had used up the life that was in her.

Fortunately, Fiona herself was the picture of health. And Cecilia was considerably healthier now; even the doctor said that they didn't need to worry about her anymore. But Hans still felt it was his duty to their mother to protect Fiona and Cecilia.

Every time something about Fiona reminded him of her mother, he got that same faraway look in his eyes—probably because he was worried. Feeling a bit embarrassed about Hans's love for her, Fiona knit her brow and laughed.

"And now you've fallen in love at first sight too? I suppose you come by it honestly."

"Hans."

"Still, whether Lord Lowell is good enough for you is another matter altogether." He scowled and made a fist, calling Giles a whippersnapper under his breath.

"If anything, I'm the one who's not good enough for Lord... Lo—for Giles."

"Nonsense! I still cannot believe his insolence. Doing such a thing in public, so carelessly!"

"Oh, um..."

So Hans did not think highly of the kiss on the cheek. *It certainly took me by surprise as well.* No matter how much he was trying to imitate Richard, Giles went too far too quickly with that move—possibly. Fiona wasn't certain. But she was embarrassed all the same.

She wasn't used to being kissed on the cheek. The only people who did such a thing were her family and Norman. *I know he was just keeping up the act, but...such behavior from him can't be good for my heart.*

His husky voice whispering in her ear. The slight warmth of his lips. He had been close enough for her to catch a faint whiff of his cedarwood cologne.

Remembering these things made warmth bloom in her face all over again. She covered her cheeks, looking away awkwardly, which only served to make Hans even more cross.

"I thought it would be another ten years still before I saw you looking like that! Why, that rascal!"

"What do you mean? What do I look like?" Had she been making a face she had never made before?

This inspired further disparagement from Hans. She was grateful he cared so much, but he would be in trouble if anyone overheard him. He was insulting the heir of the earl, after all.

Currently, Giles was a viscount, which meant that he was of higher status than her father. Compared to him, Baron Clayburn's family and all their servants were mere pawns on the board.

"I do wish you wouldn't speak so poorly of Lord Giles. Um, Hans?"

"Miss Fiona...!"

"Oh, do stop that." She handed a handkerchief to Hans, who had begun to cry.

Just then, there was a light knock at the door, and the gallery's owner, Eyser Roche, entered. "Everything all right in here?"

Under his bright blond curls, Eyser wore his usual easygoing smile and a pair of black-rimmed spectacles in front of his blue eyes. He was friendly and trustworthy, well capable of running a shop in his own name, in the city's best district—even though he was only in his mid-thirties.

Fiona mustered up a smile for him. He was both her client and her representative, after all. "Hello, Mr. Roche."

"I hope I'm not interrupting anything. Oh, Miss Fiona, did you see the letter?"

"Oh! Yes! Yes, I was just about to open it."

Hans blew his nose loudly and began to bring Roche up to speed. Roche took Fiona's seat as she went to sit at the desk. There were several documents on it requiring confirmation and a clean copy made.

There were also inquiries from people looking to purchase art and thank-you notes from others for whom she had procured and delivered paintings. She imagined the faces of the writer of each letter as she began organizing them. Dealing with customers could be difficult, of course, but Fiona gave her all to every single transaction.

To her relief, none of the correspondence required her immediate attention. She dug through the box, and at the bottom she found the letter she had been eagerly awaiting from her uncle.

Just as Fiona opened its seal, Roche said with some surprise, "Miss Fiona, you're courting Lord Lowell now?"

"Uh, yes, that's right... I think." Her heart skipped a beat and her cheeks warmed as she nodded. She was unpracticed at talking about matters of romance. Looking up and seeing her blush, Hans groaned.

"Ha ha ha! An understandable reaction to her making such a face, eh, Hans?" Roche patted Hans on the back in consolation. He was more muscular than his looks suggested; Hans audibly choked back tears of pain.

"Mr. Roche, you're bound to break his back if you don't stop."

"Whoops. My apologies. However, Hans, in all seriousness, Lord Lowell is a lucky catch. I haven't heard a single bad word from my clients about his character. You wouldn't want him for an enemy, but in general, he's not an unreasonable man."

"That's right."

Hans looked away, sullen. In all likelihood, he would take issue with any man Fiona showed interest in. Fiona couldn't help but chuckle dryly at this display of concern.

"But I'm sure you're not used to dealing with people like his friend Lord Russel. And I'd guess that things will be livelier for you from now on."

Fiona looked up from her letter at Roche again, puzzled. "What do you mean?"

"There must be droves of young women who are head over heels for Lord Lowell. Not to mention all the parents who want their daughter to be the one he chooses for his wife. I worry that they might try to come after you."

"Oh. Well, that's already happened once." Back in the palace garden, she thought it a bewildering nuisance to be mobbed by so many young ladies. But had she known from the start that this was how things would be, then she would have been better prepared. Besides... "Lord Giles had helped me out then too."

"Oh, so I've heard. But it's not as if he can be at your side at all hours of the day."

"Th-that's true."

"That reminds me, Mr. Roche," Hans said, "while I also worry about women taking their jealousy out on Miss Fiona, there's something I must ask you: Have you heard of a man named Gordon from Low Street?"

As she said the name, Roche's expression darkened. With a more dignified appearance, Hans shared what had happened at the Earl of Bancroft's home—it was crucial that they inform Mr. Roche that someone in their line of business was attempting to swindle clients with counterfeit paintings.

"I am aware of a man named Otto Gordon opening a store. But curiously, as far as I know, not a single painter directly entrusts their works to him." Roche explained that they were still in pre-opening stages and not officially open for business yet, and he had yet to join the art gallery owners' guild.

In their line of business, connections with painters and other galleries were necessities. It was rare to hear of a new gallery run by someone with no connections whatsoever, but Gordon was one such person. Even details about his history and family were a mystery.

"I have heard that people of disagreeable countenance and others hiding their faces have been seen entering Gordon's store, so I am already wary of the man," Roche continued.

"I see."

"Now I must wonder where he got that painting. Of course, there's always a possibility that he is being backed by a foreign aristocrat or there's some name lending involved. However...yes, I see. So, he's claiming to peddle Raymond's latest paintings." Roche leaned back into the sofa and re-crossed his legs, a look of disgust on his face. He folded and twisted his fingers at his chest, a habit he had developed when he was lost in thought since giving up on wearing neckties.

"It was a very convincing fake. Whoever painted it has considerable skill. I'm so glad that Lady Colet gave up on buying it," Fiona said. Someone who bought a fake for such a large sum would become a laughingstock. Miranda would be a particularly easy target, given her status as the queen of high society and her family's famous familiarity with the arts.

"I'm sure Miss Fiona could have spotted it as a fake even if he said it was a Lammert or Desmond, but to think that he claimed it was by Raymond, of all people!"

"Yes, quite unthinkable. And that man looked at Miss Fiona with such reproach when she spoke up too," Hans added.

Fiona did not falter at Hans's worried tone. "I couldn't just stand idly by!" And not only because of her sense of justice as someone affiliated with the art world. "I—I just couldn't believe that someone would try to use Uncle like that!"

In Fiona's hand was the letter from her uncle. The letter began with, "To my beloved niece" and it was signed by Reginald Raymond Bailey—the name of the very artist in question.

Fiona had been incensed but managed to hold most of it back. There was a demand for fake paintings; buyers were grateful for the opportunity to have them when they couldn't afford an original, and the painters used the exercise for practice and as a source of income. But in those cases, there was a mutual understanding between both the buyer and the seller that the painting was a replica, and of course there was a world of difference in price compared to what a genuine painting would fetch.

To help Miranda save face, Fiona suggested that perhaps it was Gordon who had been duped, but Fiona did not think that was the case. "Some people only see paintings for their monetary value, but I could tell that Gordon wasn't like that. He knew he was trying to sell Lady Colet a fake."

People who only saw paintings as a business venture got a flat look in their eyes when they viewed paintings. In Gordon's case, Fiona sensed his disdain as he looked at the painting. The memory of the honeyed words and amiable voice that he used to try to sell it made her feel sick all over again.

"Reggie will be pleased to hear that his beloved niece was able to spot a fake of his work."

"It was of a common redpoll—the same bird that Uncle painted for me!"

Common redpolls had been her mother's favorite birds. Reginald painted it for Fiona after she lost her mother.

When Fiona was a child, they told her that, due to her weak constitution, her mother had spent most of her time confined to her bed, especially in the wintertime. Out of pity for her situation, her uncle set up a birdfeeder outside of her mother's bedroom window to attract wild birds. Watching the birds was one of her mother's few pleasures during her recovery. She was especially happy whenever common redpolls came to feast.

These small birds stood out with their characteristic red plumage, which her uncle had told Fiona made it easy to spot them even if you were inside. When he gave her the painting, he said, "These birds start coming out whenever winter arrives. So, Fiona, I want you to remember that while you cannot see her now, it's only temporary—one day, you'll see your mother again."

The dead could never come back. While his words were a means to comfort her when she was a child, the bird resting on the branch in the canvas looked soft, fluffy, and happy. Her uncle rarely painted people, but in this one, he painted a small girl from behind too. The girl may have been Fiona, Cecilia...or maybe even their mother.

The painting felt so real that she thought the bird might begin to sing. Whenever Fiona looked at it, she remembered the sight of her young mother propped up with a pillow in bed, looking happy as she gazed out the window at the birds. Whenever Fiona was happy or sad, she looked at that painting. She didn't know how many times she had talked to it or been comforted by it.

Fiona lost her mother young and had few memories of her. That painting of the common redpoll was her connection to her mother—her treasure. It felt as if Gordon had stomped all over it with his fake. She had been incandescent with anger.

Of course, the only similarity was the common redpoll; the composition was completely different. For one thing, the fake didn't have the girl in it. But while she knew it was different, she couldn't bear Gordon's careless handling of it.

"A common redpoll? My…"

"Yes! How wicked."

Gordon knew that there was no record of the painting of a common redpoll. He must have chosen the subject for that reason.

"He claimed he knew someone with connections to Raymond. I fear that other fakes may be out there." Fiona fumed just remembering their conversation.

"It's possible," Hans agreed.

Roche put a contemplative hand to his chin. "Did he know that you're Baron Clayburn's daughter?"

"I didn't tell him my name. I'm sure he will find out easily once he investigates me, though."

It wasn't as if she had hidden her identity during her visit. House Clayburn's crest was even displayed on the carriage she arrived in. All that was required was for him to ask the butler or any of the servants, or even glance at the carriage.

Roche looked concerned. "We cannot say for certain what Gordon's ambitions are or whether someone's backing him. All we know for certain is that this man is dishonorable. I'll look into him again, but I want you to be careful."

"Yes, Mr. Roche is entirely right. You only just hurt your foot, and yet you went and lashed out at a man like that! I understand how you feel, but I'm very worried."

"I'm sorry for making you worry so, Hans." Fiona genuinely felt bad, but she wouldn't do anything differently if faced with the same situation again.

"If I may offer a suggestion: perhaps one of the gallery's guards should accompany you from now on? You're already acquainted with all of them."

The gallery routinely hired guards for the transport of highly valuable paintings and for exhibits. Fiona was surprised to hear Roche suggest that they hire one for her sake. "Do you think that's really necessary?"

"I hope this is only an overabundance of caution. However, we have not only Gordon to consider but also the ladies who may resent you claiming Lord Lowell for yourself. I think it would be prudent."

"Hmm, I'm still not sure. Can we wait and see if anything happens first?" Fiona knew Roche was serious, but it just didn't make sense to her. It was one thing for royalty to have bodyguards, but the mere daughter of a baron having a guard was a ridiculous notion. She feared that she would only stand out and become more of a target. Besides, she would be spending more time in Giles's company starting the following day. To have someone watch her so closely would risk revealing the truth of their relationship. "I'll make sure someone's always with me when I go out, so don't worry."

"But—"

"I promise I won't go anywhere that seems disreputable."

Roche nodded reluctantly, clearly still worried. "If you promise as much. But do contact me right away if you feel uneasy about anything. I don't know how I could face Reggie if something were to happen to you."

"I have a feeling Uncle would find the situation more amusing than anything. Oh, speaking of which, I have a letter from him." She proffered the letter in question. "I'll give it to you after I'm done."

Roche smiled. "As it so happens, he wrote to me too, for once, so don't worry. That one there is addressed solely to you." Her uncle typically wrote to them both in the same letter, but this time, evidently, he wrote to them separately. "In mine, he indicated that he's making some progress on his latest painting."

Roche looked relieved. Fiona was also happy to hear that his next painting was well underway. "Did he say what he's painting, or is it still a secret?"

"He's keeping silent on the subject, as usual. However, he said it should arrive sometime this season, so I'm sure you'll have a chance to see it while you're still here."

"Truly? I'm glad to hear that!"

Her uncle hated to be disturbed while he was working, so he kept himself locked up in his atelier. Only a select few individuals, like Fiona and Roche, were permitted entry into the room, and he never showed anyone his work until it was finished. This was partially to prevent anyone from stealing or copying his subject or composition, but mostly because he found the presence of other people annoying. He never talked about his work, nor did he have an apprentice. Therefore, so as long as he was holed up in such a far-off land, they had no idea what he was painting until the finished work arrived.

Opening a package from him felt like opening a birthday present. Fiona and Roche were discussing this when they were interrupted by a knock at the door. An employee Fiona knew well popped his head into the room.

"Excuse me, sir," the employee said to Roche before turning to Fiona. "Mrs. Bennett is here. She asked to see you as soon as I said that you're here."

A smile spread across Fiona's face at once. "We came here at just the right time, it seems."

Mrs. Bennett was the wife of wealthy businessman. She was a jolly woman of about the same age as Fiona's grandmother. Her gray hair had a lovely sheen to it, and her pretty purple eyes had a girlish sparkle. Mrs. Bennett—a fan of not only paintings, but of all works of art—was one of the gallery's most loyal customers.

"Could I ask you to attend to her?" Roche asked.

"Yes, of course!" Fiona replied, but Hans frowned and said, "That woman can talk for hours."

Mrs. Bennett came from a neighboring country but had been a resident of theirs for many years now. She was also fluent in their language; however, she missed speaking in her native language and preferred to use it whenever she was in the company of someone who knew it.

Fiona was studying foreign languages in preparation for her trip abroad, so Mrs. Bennett made for the perfect conversation partner. "It's been a while since I last had a chance to practice. It's not like we're going to go out walking anywhere, so it should be okay, right?"

"Be that as it may, you promised me that you would work for only an hour and a half today."

Hans intended to hold Fiona to her promise. But while Roche could speak many languages, and many of his employees were proficient as well, it seemed that Mrs. Bennett felt more relaxed talking with another woman. She was glad whenever Fiona was in and had a habit of talking with her for a very long time.

"But, Hans, I rarely get a chance to practice. At this rate, I'm going to forget my pronunciation."

Not only that, but Mrs. Bennett would often buy something during their conversations. Besides, Fiona liked her personality and took great interest in Mrs. Bennett's tales of life abroad and of the store she ran. She was as valuable a source of information as Olga since Fiona rarely went to any parties.

"Hans, please, consider this a request from me as well," said Roche.

"I guess I have no choice but to allow it," Hans caved with a reluctant sigh. "However, you must warn her that you're injured and cannot talk for long."

"I will."

"I'll stay here and organize the documents, then. Please keep an eye on Miss Fiona for me, Mr. Roche."

"Keep an eye on me? Hans! We're only going to be inside the store." She felt that her late mother was half the reason he still treated her as a child, so she couldn't flat-out refuse him, but there were times when his overprotective ways grated on her nerves.

Judging from his forced smile, Roche understood how she felt. "Ha ha! Just leave her to me. Let us be off then."

"All right." Fiona put the letter from her uncle in her pocket and headed out to the front of the store.

The day after the prince's party at the royal palace, around the time that Fiona was in her carriage on her way to return the cuff link, Lord Richard Russel arrived at the Earl of Bancroft's residence.

"So, about your missing cuff link," Richard began as soon as the servant finished serving tea and left the room. Giles was clearly more interested in hearing what Richard found out than he was in the tea. "I checked with the palace's head maid and the grand chamberlain himself, and I even took the time to search for it in the garden, but no one's found it. Any leads on your end?"

"None. Perhaps a cleaner picked it up and is keeping it hidden."

"Well, I can't say it's not a possibility." Richard shook his head, discontented.

Giles raised his hands slightly in a placatory gesture. "I'm sorry. It's not that I doubt your eyes, or the people employed at the castle."

"Don't worry about it. I'd be panicking too if I lost something with my crest on it."

Giles had realized one of his cuff links was missing just after they returned to the main hall from the garden where they had sought refuge. He immediately retraced his steps, but it was difficult to find a small, black accessory at night—even with the area well-illuminated. He had no choice but to depart the castle and leave trusted people to search in his stead.

That morning, Giles entrusted the palace search to Richard, who had contacts in the castle, while he searched the carriage and his house—just in case. He even turned the clothes he wore to the celebration inside out but to no avail. He feared that he truly must've lost it at the castle.

Losing a cuff link wasn't ever a good thing, but he wouldn't be going to such lengths to find a regular cuff link. He was frantic because the cuff link in question had his crest on it. He couldn't just give up on it; if it found its way into the wrong hands, someone could use it with bad intentions.

"I think it fell off because I readjusted it myself." If he had just let it be, then surely it wouldn't have fallen off. But after obligatory dances with several women, all of whom clung closer to him than necessary, his clothes wound up in a state of disarray. Giles removed the cuff link while attempting to tidy his appearance.

"Since it hasn't turned up after this much searching, it's likely that someone has it in their possession," Richard said.

"You think so?"

If, during their undesirable encounter with the women in the garden, one of Giles's pursuers had forced her way close to him and snatched it in the confusion... Giles's expression turned grim. Even Richard looked perturbed.

"I presume it would be preferable to you if they only try to extort you."

"Yeah."

When someone of the opposite sex was in possession of one's house's crest, the implication was typically that that person was one's beloved or fiancée. Only the person who had the cuff link knew for certain whether they had simply picked it up or stolen it, but a woman in possession of that crest could proclaim herself Giles's partner. If she told people that Giles gave it to her, it would be difficult to make her recant before rumors spread.

Rumors with evidence to back them up were automatically accepted as truth, even when they were lies. Giles's parents were already vexed at him for declining every potential match they presented. If such a rumor reached their ears... Giles didn't even want to think about it.

"It'll be a straight shot all the way to the altar with you. Courtney's Cathedral will be waiting to ring the marriage bells just for you."

"I do wish you wouldn't read my mind like that."

"I don't have to read your mind to know what you're thinking. But enough with the jokes. Can you remember who was there last night?"

Giles frowned contemplatively as he tried to recall who one woman from the garden was. "That one we've seen on multiple occasions."

"Hey now, it was Lady Caroline in the lead. The Earl of Burleigh's daughter—the one with the curly hair?"

She was lauded for her beauty. But Giles put a hand to his chin, squinting as he continued to search his memories. "There were two with curly hair. The loud one and the one who made a big fuss. Which one are you referring to?"

"That's how you remember them?" Richard heaved an exaggerated sigh. Despite Richard's exasperated look, he knew that Giles didn't care to remember people he wasn't interested in. He remembered only that seeing them put him on guard. "Fine. Leave remembering all the members of the lady army to me."

"That'd be a big help. Thanks."

Still, Richard scowled with some annoyance. "There's one I don't know—the one we saw first."

"Who?"

"The girl Lady Caroline nearly knocked over. She arrived just before Lady Caroline. We spoke with her a little."

It had been a quarrel between women. Or perhaps it was better to say that the first woman was attacked head-on, without provocation. It wasn't that Giles didn't remember her—he had just unconsciously excluded her from the list of possible suspects. The thought didn't even occur to him until Richard brought her up.

"You even caught her before she fell. Don't tell me you don't remember her?"

"No, how could I forget? But she's not like them."

She seemed modest without any of the tenacity that the other women who were after the seat of countess displayed. Giles felt nothing unpleasant toward her, which was rare for him when it came to young women. If all the ladies were like her, he wouldn't have such an aversion to women.

Giles crossed his arms as he thought bitterly. *They say time heals all wounds, but it's certainly not working for me.* In their long friendship, he had never told Richard the true reason he rejected women and, by extension, marriage. He longed to forget what had happened, but he just couldn't. He shook his head, trying to push the intrusive thoughts away, and took a sip of his tea, which was still warm.

"Well, it really did seem like she just happened to be passing by. She didn't even seem to know who either of us were."

"Yeah."

She had greeted them like any other ordinary people you might happen upon in the street. If they weren't interrupted, she likely would've just wished them a pleasant evening after another minute of chatting and then been on her way.

As Giles and Richard were among the most famous people in high society, strangers rarely conducted themselves in such an easygoing manner when speaking with them. Perhaps it sounded like egotism, but it was the truth.

She had such slender shoulders, Giles thought. The woman had looked stunned, baffled as to how she was pushed or that she was in Giles's arms. It was a breath of fresh air how, even though he held her, all she did was blink at him without a hint of hunger or lust in her eyes.

"Which reminds me—she didn't stop for you?"

"So it seemed." Maybe she had just ignored him. Back in the garden, she started walking away after giving another proper curtsy, but it looked like she might've been favoring one of her legs... Regardless, she didn't look back.

"I wonder what family she's from. Ugh, it's too bad. If only we could have talked to her a bit longer."

"You're curious about her?"

"I thought about her all night, but I just couldn't place who she is. It's rare that we go to a party where there's a woman who doesn't know me, and I don't know her."

"You really do always have women on your mind, Rick."

"Yesterday was the prince's debut, so it's not like that could've been her debut into society." Richard took pride in knowing every eligible young lady of high society, regardless of her peerage. He seemed shocked to have found a woman he didn't know.

An uncomfortable feeling welled up in Giles's chest at hearing that his friend had thought about her all night, but he shrugged it off. "Well, based on my experience, she wasn't the kind of girl who's interested in the title of countess and the like. I doubt she had any interest in your cuff link, so I agree that we can probably just let her be."

"Which means that she'd have no interest in one of your crests either."

"What? Are you trying to compete with me?" Richard had no intention of handing one of his crests over, but he didn't like the idea of a woman refusing it either. He and Giles were close enough to poke fun at each other like this, and it helped to relieve the tension a bit. "I'll try asking the ladies to help look for it too, in a roundabout way. But Gil, I think it would be best to tell your father about this."

"I suppose you're right," Giles reluctantly agreed. They would need to take measures to ensure the crest wouldn't be misused. Giles grew up under the pressure of his father's expectations, so it weighed heavily on him to have to confess his mistake.

"I'm sure we'll find it soon." Richard patted Giles's shoulder sympathetically. "I'll go speak to Lady Caroline right away, so don't worry."

"I'm in your debt."

"And I'm in yours," Richard said as he stood up from the sofa.

Just then, there was a knock at the door. After receiving permission to enter, the head butler, Dalton, came in with a letter in hand. "I apologize for interrupting your conversation. There's a lady here who asked that you read this, my lord."

"A lady?"

Many women came calling to see if they could suss out any weaknesses in the future Earl of Bancroft's armor. Fed up with it all, Giles had instructed his butler to flatly reject any woman who came calling without a prior appointment.

Dalton was aware that the only person Giles was planning to meet with today was Richard. Giles gave the butler who had served his family for decades a quizzical look when he held out a tray containing two envelopes.

"She has no appointment, but she has a personal reference letter from Lord Talbott himself, so I thought it best to pass this on just in case."

"What?" Lord Talbott was the former prime minister. He had retired a year prior due to his age, but he still held powerful sway in the political world. On multiple occasions, Giles's father had said that Lord Talbott was unique, and not a man to make an enemy of. With a letter from Lord Talbott himself, it didn't matter whether this lady was young or if she had a prior appointment.

"She said her name is Fiona Clayburn, the daughter of Baron Clayburn."

"Clayburn? I've heard the name before." They were a long line, but that was all—there was nothing noteworthy about the family. In fact, they were the kind of simple folk who spent more time at their fief than in the capital. They held no important post and the earl's family had no relation to them.

All Giles knew of them was the face and name of the current baron, and that his fief had suffered from recent torrential rains. If the baron asked for a meeting with Giles's father, he would likely request some kind of assistance or for Giles to put in a good word for him. But it was a different matter altogether with his daughter calling on Giles.

He glanced at Richard and found him with a contemplative hand to his chin. "I've never met her before either. However, hmm, I recall the baron having two daughters."

"You really do know every woman."

"One of them has yet to make her debut in high society. Oh, then perhaps..."

Giles left Richard to his pondering and asked Dalton about the purpose of Miss Clayburn's visit.

"She claims to be looking for someone. She asked that you read her letter for more details."

"Ah, I see." The earl's family had a wide range of connections; it was not unusual for anyone in their position to request notarized assistance.

He suspected that his visitor must be looking for a man, since she asked for him and not his mother. *But at a time like this?* Truthfully, Giles was not in an obliging mood, but he did feel some sympathy for Miss Clayburn given that he, too, was in search of something. For this reason, he decided not to reject her request outright.

Giles looked up again and met Richard's gaze. As it turned out, Richard had already picked up the letter of introduction.

He waved the envelope at Giles and said, "Don't worry, the letter is genuine. And it's not like you can turn away a visitor with an introduction from Lord Talbott. Why don't you give the other letter a read?"

He had a point. Giles opened the letter and, after a moment, said, "Oh my."

There was only a single sentence written on the plain paper. Giles stared at the sentence in shock. It read, "Do you know who the owner of the star in the evening sky is?"

His cuff links were made of black agate. The face of them was made of onyx, which looked like the night sky, with his crest engraved on it. The backing was decorated with a single star-shaped diamond.

Richard peeked at the letter with a raised eyebrow and then hit Giles on the back. "Oh! You've found it!"

"Bring her in," Giles said after a moment. "No, wait, I'll go myself. I'm guessing she's in the parlor?"

"She is waiting in the entrance hall."

"In the hall?" Even if she were a sudden caller of a lower rank, it wouldn't do to leave a woman with a letter from the former prime minister waiting by the front door.

Dalton cast his eyes down, sensing Giles's thoughts. "I invited her into the parlor, but she said that if you did not understand the meaning of the letter, then she would leave without meeting you."

Giles was surprised again. That meant she only wanted to see whoever was the owner of the cuff link—not necessarily

Giles Bancroft. "Very well then. I'll bring her to the parlor on the second floor."

"Very good, my lord."

Giles ordered Dalton to have the room prepared. The butler bowed courteously and then left.

"Care to join us in the parlor?" Giles asked Rick.

"Can I?"

"I would prefer if you did."

Giles was relieved—it sounded like she really did have his cuff link—but she was still a woman. He couldn't help but have some anxiety about the situation. From the way the letter was written, it didn't sound like she had designs on him personally, but he couldn't be certain whether she was merely hiding her true intentions. There had been times in the past when a woman who seemed disinterested in him completely changed her demeanor, the moment she had him alone.

Giles urged Richard to head to the parlor while he went to meet their guest in the entrance hall. As he approached the stairs, he heard pleasant chatter.

"Oh my, is that true, Miss?"

"Yes. The fountain had three tiers and at the top was a pretty angel. It was in the queen's garden."

He peered over the banister to see a woman wearing a modest-colored dress speaking with two of his family's maids below.

"So, you mean that the painting at the end there...?"

"It very well could have been the model for it."

"My!"

She was the daughter of a baron, and they were servants—
yet here they were, talking like good friends. Giles had never
seen his father, let alone his mother or older sister, chat with
the servants like this. Moreover, the elderly servant who stood
behind the young woman looked at her more like a beloved
granddaughter than with the reverence one would normally
show for his master.

Finding it all quite unusual, Giles began to descend the stairs.
The maids noticed the sound of his footsteps, gave an awkward
apology, and made a hasty exit. The woman thanked them as
they rushed away, then turned to face Giles as he came down
the stairs.

Had he taken the time to think about it calmly he might've
surmised as much, but Giles was shocked to find that he already
knew his visitor. *She's the woman from last night.*

Still, he didn't let his surprise show. He stood before her and
did his best to greet her in a composed manner. "You're Miss
Clayburn, I take it? I apologize for my servants' discourtesy."

"Not at all. It was I who addressed them first. Please do not
find fault with them." She explained that she had imposed on
them for a bit of small talk. Giles had no recourse but to agree
to her request not to blame the maids. "I am Fiona Clayburn.
I apologize for calling upon you so unexpectedly."

This woman, whom he had held in his arms for the briefest
moment, gave a well-practiced, proper curtsy. She was dressed
modestly, but she carried herself with grace—perhaps even more
so than his sister or mother, who reigned over high society.

Giles shook his head a little to clear his thoughts. "And I am Giles Bancroft."

Even Richard didn't know this woman, who likely had no interest in keeping his cuff link. In the light of day, he could see that her looks were ordinary. Her words were as plain as her dress and, curiously, she didn't make much of a lasting impression.

Why does she—? No, there's no need to wonder. It must have happened when she was about to fall. Was that fall an accident, or intentional? He regarded her carefully, but her tone carried no hint of bewilderment, nor did her eyes show any glint of change.

If she was here with a guilty conscience, he didn't think she could remain so calm, especially not given how inexperienced she must've been in the ways of social maneuvering. Besides, she looked at him without a hint of flirtation.

It had been far too long since he last had a chance to speak with a young woman who didn't see him as a trophy for the taking.

TRUE LOVE Fades Away When the Contract Ends

One Star in the Night Sky

CHAPTER 6

Clandestine Conversations Happen at the Park

THE MORNING AFTER FIONA'S VISIT to the Bancroft estate, Baron Clayburn found himself flabbergasted at the punctual arrival of their expected guest. "L-Lord Lowell?! You're r-r-r-really him?"

"I apologize for calling on you so early in the morning. I have an engagement with Fiona today. Are you all right, Lord Clayburn?"

"Y-y-yes! I'm fine! My apologies! An engagement? W-with Fiona?" He had heard of the viscount's expected visit, but thought it was some kind of mistake. Hans, who was currently watching his floundering master from a distance, had given him a report of the previous day's events. But never in his wildest dreams did the baron believe that the heir to the Earl of Bancroft might actually show up at his home. "H-Hans! Where is Fiona?"

"I'm right here, Father."

"Ah, Fiona, my dear! What is the meaning of this?" The sight of his beloved daughter dressed to go out only made the baron more confused.

There were dark circles under Fiona's eyes, and she looked pale.

Cecilia, summoned by the commotion, rushed to her sister's side when she saw how unwell Fiona looked. "Sister, do you have a fever or a cold? Or does your stomach ache?"

"What's gotten into you? Your vitality has always been your most defining feature!"

"Please calm yourselves, both of you. I'm fine. You're just being so loud, Father."

"I-I apologize."

Both father and sister ignored Giles to crowd around Fiona. Their entrance hall was not large, and so the whole scene felt chaotic.

Fiona sensed that she wouldn't be allowed to go out at all if things continued in this manner. Pressing a hand to her forehead, she exchanged a look with Giles, pleading him to help her out by giving a proper greeting to the head of her family.

Thankfully, he was able to intuit her meaning. "I apologize for interrupting, Lord Clayburn. May I please invite your daughter out today?"

"Huh? Oh, uh, y-yes?"

"I shall head out, then. Hans, please look after Father and Cecilia for me."

Leaving Hans to deal with her astonished sister and her father, who continued to gape like fish, Fiona pushed Giles out the door. She breathed a sigh of relief when it shut behind her, and they started down the stairs.

"I'm sorry about that. They don't normally act that way." *I've never seen Father behave like that before. I guess it was the shock of the next Earl of Bancroft visiting our home.*

Despite her apology, Fiona remained unaware that the primary reason for her father's distress was that a man was calling on her.

"Don't worry, I don't mind. However, you do seem unwell."

"I was up all night. I just need some proper sleep."

"Why couldn't you sleep?"

"I was reading."

"Reading?" Giles's look of concern wasn't an act. Fiona lightly covered her eyes with her fingers to shield them from the bright rays of the sun. The sight of him and the brightness of the sun were both too much for her tired eyes.

"If I'm being honest: I don't know how to act as someone's partner, so I was reading novels in the hope that they might give me some idea."

"Ah, I see."

Fiona had started working through the pile of romance novels from her friend Olga, and the next thing she knew, it was dawn. Even though she knew she should sleep, her hands just wouldn't stop turning the pages.

A breeze blew past, and something touched her cheek soothingly. She uncovered her eyes and found Giles looking at her closely, his hand on her cheek. "Huh?"

"You're looking a little better now that we're outside, but please be sure to tell me if you truly feel unwell."

"Oh, thank you." The brush of the backs of his fingers against her cheek caught her off guard. Suddenly she felt wide awake.

Before she could recover her composure, he helped her to smoothly board the waiting carriage. It was a small, canopied, two-wheeled carriage that shone in the bright sun; led by an intelligent-looking bay horse that waited obediently for their arrival. Inside, the seats were covered in high-quality leather. They felt too luxurious for a carriage; it made Fiona aware of just how much power the earl's family had.

Giles drove the carriage, so it truly had no passengers but Giles and Fiona. Unlike Fiona, who wore a dress that she deemed a safe choice, Giles looked sophisticated and stylish in his light clothing. The pin holding his cravat in place was made of sapphire, which brought out his eyes. With his handsome features, he was a lovely vision to behold.

This shouldn't only be occurring to me now, but I can't believe I was so brazen as to ask someone like him to pretend to be my lover. She had been caught up in the possibilities suggested by Richard's plan, but it was still an unthinkable thing for a plain girl like her to have asked for. She must've been desperate.

But even a day later, she couldn't come up with a better idea. And the fact that Giles came to pick her up as promised likely meant that he had no intention of going back on his word.

I guess I'll have to try my best to be his match, she vowed to herself as she heard the wheels of the carriage begin to turn. The last thing she wanted was for him to regret this arrangement because he was disappointed in her.

Giles was a skilled driver, so she had no apprehensions about riding with him. Was the man perfect at everything?

Fiona asked after their destination, and he told her they would go to the park at the center of the castle town. "You mean where the botanical garden is?"

"That's right. I thought we could discuss things during the drive. We don't have to worry about any eavesdropping, and a great number of people will be able to see us together. Or, at least, that's what Rick suggested."

They needed their courtship to be public knowledge, but no one besides the three of them could ever find out that it was an act. At home, they would have to deal with the prying eyes of family and servants. At shops outdoors, any number of people might listen in on their conversation. But in the carriage, so long as they didn't speak too loudly, no one would hear them—and anyone who saw them would assume they were courting. The carriage would allow them to be both public and discreet, killing two birds with one stone.

"Richard said that we need to make sure as many people know about us as possible before this weekend's ball."

"That makes sense."

Richard suggested that their plan to appear intimate at the party would be more effective if everyone were already talking about them. The man truly was a master at social maneuvering.

Giles, however, seemed dubious. "Do you think so?"

"I do think he's right. I mean, look around."

It was still morning, but plenty of people were out and

about. Most of them turned around to get a peek at the passing carriage—or rather at Giles, who was quite the local celebrity.

"Well, I suppose we'll be able to judge the true worth of his counsel at the ball," Giles mused skeptically, as he gave a small shake of his head.

While he knew the power gossip could have, it seemed he was not well-versed in utilizing it to his own advantage. *He's probably been focused on trying to* avoid *rumors about himself. I feel bad for him.*

It wasn't easy being popular. Fiona thought she could never understand how difficult it was to be so attractive.

"I was up late myself last night, speaking with Rick."

"Oh?"

"He thoroughly lectured me on how to conduct myself with a lady."

Uh, I think that actually makes me feel more worried, not less. After all, Giles's attempts to imitate his friend the previous night had left her shaken.

All the novels she'd spent the night reading had mentioned similar emotions, so she knew this was just how it was with romance. However, she had her limits.

Mildly, she asked, "Um, Lord Giles? Don't you think it might prove difficult to emulate Lord Russel?"

A slight frown crossed Giles's face. "But among my friends, Rick has the most experience with women. It's also easy for me to think of how he might act in different situations. And we don't have enough time for me to study how other men behave."

Fiona had the impression that Giles had repeated this argument to himself many times over by now.

"It would be most efficient for me to copy him."

"But you two are so..."

"I cannot pretend to know what you think of me, but Rick said it would be ideal for me to act in ways that I do not normally."

In some of the novels, falling in love brought out hidden parts of a character's personality and made them behave in unexpected ways. She could understand where Rick was coming from, but it still made her worry. "It won't make you uncomfortable?"

"Uncomfortable?"

"I've heard that you have an aversion to women. Won't having to touch me be a burden on you?" He had escorted her, kissed her on the cheek, and just moments before, caressed her face. She had nearly forgotten in the moment, because of how naturally he touched her, but it was all an act so that Giles could avoid marriage. His touching her wasn't because of something he felt inside. "There's no need for you to force yourself to do something that you find physically repulsive. You could just do the movements but not actually touch me, and angle it so that it's not obvious."

She was certain that he would want minimal physical contact, including when he had to escort her. Fiona thought her suggestion was reasonable—she wanted to stop herself from mistaking the means for the end—but her words brought a serious expression back to Giles's face. He sunk into silence as he turned to face the road again.

Huh? What's gotten into him? Fiona was bewildered by the sudden heaviness between them.

Still looking ahead, Giles asked, "Does my touch make you uncomfortable?"

"Well...no." Giles escorting her and kissing her cheek had taken her by surprise, but she didn't dislike it; nor did she find it uncomfortable. However, she felt that she hadn't experienced joy from it either. In the novels, the heroines were delighted at their love interest's touch; they never felt bewildered by it. This was why Fiona didn't quite understand how to describe what it was that she was feeling. "I do not mind if you touch me. However, I shall endeavor not to cling to you, so please be at ease on that point."

After a pause, Giles said, "Thank you."

Even if she was playing the part of his beloved, he was sure to be repulsed by her clinging to him. At least, that was what she had assumed. But strangely, Giles's mood had only soured. *Have I wounded his pride? I mean, even he admitted that women make him uncomfortable. Ugh, I just can't understand him.*

Things had been so harmonious between them up until that point. Fiona couldn't understand his sudden change in mood, but she refused to back down and let things stand as they were. "Have I said something that offends you?"

There was another pause. "Of course not."

"But, um, please...tell me if there's something troubling you. I have no experience with courtship myself, so this is all brand new for me as well. I wouldn't like to be the cause of your unhappiness."

When she thought about it, they had only known each other for three days. They were of different ages, sexes, and upbringings; naturally there was much they didn't know about one another. Fiona wanted them to communicate and tell each other what they really wanted, so that they could bridge the distance and discord between them.

Fiona stumbled her way through explaining these thoughts to Giles, who listened in silence. "We are going to be telling all kinds of lies to other people from now on, after all."

"Yes, I suppose."

"So, at the very least, I would like to not have any lies between us."

That declaration made Giles finally look at her again.

They were about to carry out a high-handed act for their own selfish reasons. Perhaps she was being hypocritical to soothe her own conscience, but she was sincere in thinking that, at the very least, she and Giles should be honest with one another.

"If there's something you don't like, I would prefer that you tell me so we can work out a solution together."

Hearing this, a small smile tugged at the corners of his lips. He looked forward again, lightly swinging the reins to usher the horses on. "So no lies or forcing ourselves into uncomfortable situations. We shall respect one another. Those are the conditions for us pretending to be a couple. Is that correct?"

"That is what I would like."

"Just to confirm, then, my touch does not upset you?"

Fiona nodded. "Correct." When Giles touched her, she didn't feel the revulsion she experienced when serving rude customers at the gallery or dancing with impolite men at parties. She could say that for certain.

"Then there's no problem. However, I would prefer it if you also put in the effort to act as my beloved, so that we seem like an ordinary couple—taking care not to be overly excessive about it, of course."

"You'll tell me if I take things too far?"

"I promise I shall." Giles smiled contentedly, bringing an answering smile to Fiona's face.

Soon thereafter, they arrived at the park. The carriage proceeded down a lane that traced the edge of the large pond. The trees had fresh verdure, and waterfowl played on the clear surface of the water. It was a perfect day for a walk.

Many people were in the park to enjoy a morning of relaxation. Some even slowed their carriages to get a good, long look at Fiona and Giles as they passed. They pretended not to notice, hoping to appear to be happily lost in their own little world.

"By the way, what kind of novels were you reading?"

"Olga—ah, she's the friend who gave me the books—loves dramatic tales. But all of them were about princesses and pirate queens, so I couldn't quite use those for reference," Fiona confided, which made Giles chuckle.

"Ha-ha! I suppose not."

After their meeting at his residence, she knew the Icy Scion to be just another person. Now she found herself less and less startled by his displays of emotion, though they were still rare enough to take her aback—not that she would let it show or point it out to him.

The heroines of Olga's novels were of social standing or positions quite different from her own. Having grown up running around the verdant fields of their countryside fief, Fiona knew nothing of palace intrigue or battles on the rough seas. Still, she could understand the characters' feelings, which made the books engaging to read...and which had landed her in her current sleepless condition.

"But there were some things in them I think I can copy," she continued. "It seems that when women fall in love, they usually change how they dress and how they do their hair."

"Is that so?"

Girls who dressed in a more rustic fashion would abruptly change their appearance, even curling their hair in a manner befitting a princess. This kind of brilliant transformation happened in many of the books. In all honesty, though, Fiona was unconvinced that such a transformation would be all that dramatic. A person could change her dress or hair, but it wouldn't change her facial features or eye color. A beautiful woman was a beautiful woman, no matter what she wore or what color her hair was. Fiona suspected it was a matter of the characters having always been beautiful, and the people around them simply not seeing it.

Moreover, she doubted that changing her clothes alone would significantly alter the impression she left on people—after all, she was ordinary and easily forgettable. It would be a meaningful gesture to do so, though, a way to play her part as "the future Earl of Bancroft's beloved." In other words, she would be wearing a costume.

Giles listened with great interest as Fiona explained her thoughts. "So I was thinking of stopping by my friend's dress-making shop."

"Let's go together."

"I'll be just fine by myself." She was surprised, not having expected him to make such an offer.

But Giles was nonchalant when he replied, "Rick told me that I should accompany you when you go shopping, whether it's for clothes or jewels. Did that not happen in your novels?"

"Oh... Now that you mention it, the couples did go shopping together a lot."

Giles nodded, satisfied that his point was made, and it was decided that they would go to the shop together.

"I was planning to go tomorrow. Are you free?"

"What time?"

As it so happened, the time she suggested was exactly when Parliament would adjourn. This astounding coincidence made it seem like they had planned for it in advance. Fiona had no reason to decline, so they quickly settled on a meeting place.

Imitating Richard, and the novels, was the safest course of action. But Fiona still had to gear herself up to do it. Nevertheless...

"Lord Russel really is knowledgeable about how men should conduct themselves with women. I'm impressed."

"I knew he was used to courtship, but I was surprised myself at just how knowledgeable he really is. Rick also said that we should meet and do things together every day."

"But don't you have Parliament and other social obligations to attend to?"

The capital's social season was scheduled around Parliament. Her father had attended this morning as well and would be busy late into the evening finishing his manuscripts. The nightly parties were actually meant as opportunities for behind-the-scenes maneuvering and networking. In short, the social season was an extension of their work. Fiona could only assume that, being of a higher rank than her father, Giles was incredibly busy. She had no desire to interfere with his work.

"My schedule is far more flexible, so I'll do what I can to match yours."

"Are you sure? It would certainly be helpful for me."

"Yes. Few of the things I do for my work require scheduling around anyone else." Fiona thought that cooperating with him in this way was the obvious move, since they were both in this scheme together, but Giles seemed surprised. *Did I say something weird again?* "Oh, but there will be times when I do have my own obligations—such as when I have negotiations to conduct or deliveries to oversee."

"That's fine. You don't need to go so far out of your way to match my schedule. You have important work to do too."

Important work.

He said the words so matter-of-factly that Fiona was at a momentary loss for words. "Um...yes. Thank you."

Typically, people looked upon women of noble birth who worked outside of the house with disdain. Fiona's father and even

Hans approved of her working, but this was the first time anyone had shown an understanding and respect for her work. *What's gotten into me? I feel so happy right now.*

She must've been staring at his profile. Giles noticed her gaze and smiled. He turned to look at her. "Please do not feel that you have to rearrange your obligations for my sake."

"Thank you."

Fiona sighed in relief: it seemed she had managed to remove yet another layer of the armor around his heart. They may have decided to do this together, but it was clear that Giles was still apprehensive.

Fiona glanced around at their surroundings and found a great deal of attention being paid to their carriage in the busy park. Someone was even pointing at them; when they noticed her looking, they quickly turned away. "It seems we're garnering attention."

"What do you know? Rick was ri—"

Just then, one of the wheels went over a stone. The carriage lurched up, bringing Fiona even closer to Giles. Her hand landed on his muscular thigh for support and her head bumped into the top of his shoulder.

At the sight of her seemingly coquettish leaning against him, several women walking down the path simultaneously unfolded their fans and huddled together.

"Wow, incredible..." Fiona breathed.

"That seemed rather effective," Giles said.

Fiona nodded, agreeing with his assessment. She had no doubt that rumors would be flying about town at this rate.

Giles had to attend Parliament, so she didn't want to waste what time he had. She decided to stop caring about what everyone else was doing and focus on continuing their planning. At present, their first objective was the ball to be held at the Earl of Burleigh's estate on the upcoming weekend. It was the home of the very woman who was so keen on Giles. They came up with strategies to ensure that she got a full view of their intimacy, so that she would finally give up on him.

"I've never been to a ball at an earl's residence before."

"They're not so different from any other ball, aside from the attendees. However, Fiona, we'll have to dance. How is your ankle doing?"

"It was just a light sprain. I'm planning to remove the bandage tomorrow."

"I see. That's good, then." However, dancing the quadrille might make it ache a little. It was a dance where multiple couples changed partners. Normally, Fiona enjoyed that kind of dance; surely dancing it once wouldn't hurt her too much. "Also, we shall only dance waltzes."

"What?"

"We shall not dance any reels or quadrille."

"O-oh?" Fiona wondered if he had read her mind.

Waltzes were only danced together. They were meant for couples, married or unmarried. And Giles was saying they would only dance to those. *I guess that would make us appear all the more intimate, and make it harder for people to find us out.* The more they had to socialize with other people, the more they risked someone seeing through their act.

They needed to keep contact with others to the bare minimum, then. Moreover, Richard had ordered them to keep up the appearance that they only had eyes for each other, probably to ensure that they didn't accidentally let something slip.

Giles misinterpreted Fiona's bewilderment. "Are you not good at waltzes?"

"I can do the steps, more or less. However, I do not have enough experience actually dancing one to know if I am bad at it."

Since Fiona had never proactively hunted for a potential fiancé, she had very little experience with these kinds of parties. The only people with whom she had ever danced a waltz were her father, her uncle, and Norman.

She imagined that if they did the waltz in the traditional way instead of what might be in fashion nowadays, she could pull it off, but it might be difficult to achieve the level Giles would be hoping for.

After she communicated these worries, Giles asked not about dances but with whom she had experience dancing. "Who's Norman?"

"My childhood friend. The man my father was planning to betroth me to."

"Ah, that one."

"Yes. At the party at the palace the other night, he was the only one I danced with." She had been distracted and even stepped on his feet as they danced. Norman laughed it off, but she felt bad for stepping on him so many times.

Wait, that party was only the day before yesterday, wasn't it? So many things have happened since then that it feels like months ago. Fiona stared off into the distance as she recalled everything that had happened the past couple of days. Then she noticed Giles's frown. "Is something wrong?"

After a moment, he said, "Fiona, you must not dance with him from now on. I am sure that there will be men who invite you to dance this weekend, but you must decline them as well."

"But wouldn't that be rude?"

Fiona was rarely invited to dance at parties. She normally spent the time chatting animatedly with her friends. But while no one showed any interest in Fiona Clayburn, they would certainly be interested in "Giles Bancroft's sweetheart."

Fiona wanted to avoid trouble. While she was good at business negotiations for paintings, she was not so skilled at aristocratic maneuvering. It would be best if she didn't dance with anyone if she didn't have to, but it was a different issue altogether if someone were to invite her to dance.

"If you must, then I will choose your partner. Otherwise, you are to dance with no one but me."

Giles didn't sound like he was joking, which made Fiona's breath catch in her throat. For some reason, the way he phrased it made it sound like he wanted her all for himself. She knew that couldn't be the case, but she felt it strange that she might even think that.

"Hee hee, another piece of advice from Lord Russel, I take it."

"No, he didn't—" Giles stopped, seeming surprised at himself. "What I meant was, um—"

Fiona interrupted his flustered attempt to correct himself. "It's all right. Don't worry, I'll only dance with you."

Giles seemed relieved. He looked toward the road again and adjusted his grasp on the reins. "Yes. That would be good."

They both went silent then. A breeze blew across the surface of the water. *This whole pretending to be in love thing might be more difficult than I anticipated.*

It was all just a ruse, but there was some uncomfortable, creeping feeling in her heart. She gazed at Giles's hands and decided that she would finish reading the remaining novels when she got home.

They planned on a few more dates and came up with some extra backstory for themselves before they left the park. Their short time in the park was so eventful that Fiona felt her head was full to bursting with thoughts, and it wasn't even noon yet. They only needed to turn the corner and proceed down the street to arrive at the Clayburns' townhouse, but it was then that Fiona suddenly remembered something important.

"Oh yes, what did you want to do about the contract? Would you like me to prepare it?"

"What contract?" Giles asked. Fiona had indeed proposed signing a legal document when she entreated Giles to pretend to be her beau. She thought it an obvious necessity to prevent either of them from going back on their agreement or breaching their established rules. But Giles gave her another strange look as he said, "You did mention something like that yesterday, didn't you? I'm guessing it's a habit from your job to be able to speak of contracts so naturally?"

"It doesn't guarantee things will go flawlessly, but it's better to have one—just to be safe."

Fiona could see that insisting upon a written contract might imply that she didn't have trust in their verbal agreement—hardly something that would endear her to Giles. But the first thing Roche taught her when she began working for her uncle was the importance of contracts. Contracts were a form of self-defense, yes, but they also increased customer satisfaction by minimizing misunderstandings about the product and its handling.

Surely pretending to be in love was not so different from buying and selling paintings.

"While I agree it would be better to have a contract, it would leave a paper trail that could potentially be discovered."

"Oh!"

Giles tapped his temple. "That's why I did everything I could to commit Rick's advice to memory and took no notes."

He was right. It would not do to leave physical evidence of their secret arrangement. "What should we do instead?"

There would be nothing but problems if one of them were to alter their agreement. Naturally, Fiona had no intentions of going back on her word, but she doubted either of them could rest easy without something physical to prove the promise they made.

"I'm more worried about how I was unable to make a proper introduction to Baron Clayburn than I am about a contract."

"Don't worry about that. I doubt he would hear a single word you might say right now."

It had been awful to see her father so shaken up that morning. She made excuses, but he was normally a much more dignified sort of man. Her father had no desire to move up in the world and kept socializing with other nobles to a minimum; he didn't see it as important.

He was aware that the lives of the higher classes, like royalty, earls, and marquises, were distant from their own. Fiona was sure that one the reasons he could not recover himself in front of the heir of an earl, even one as young as Giles, was because her father was unaccustomed to dealing with high-ranking nobles.

Giles was apologetic for not being able to introduce himself properly, but in fact it was her father who had been impolite.

"But I kind of doubt that me taking you out like this will be enough for him to call off the engagement to your childhood friend." Giles was worried that they hadn't shown her father conclusive evidence of their relationship yet.

It relieved Fiona to hear that he was concerned for not only his own situation but hers as well. "Me too. However, he did seem a bit—no, more than that—quite shaken by the event. I'll wait until it's the right time to explain the whole situation to him. It should be okay then."

"You think so?"

"Yes. Truly, I'm so sorry about what happened—"

"Don't worry about it," Giles said, heading off her apology. After a pause, he continued, "Your family seems quite close."

It felt as if he were admitting that his own family wasn't. Fiona was curious about his relationship with his parents, but she found herself unable to ask. *All families have their individual situations.*

Their finances aside, the Clayburns were all exceedingly close to one another. They enjoyed harmonious relations with the citizens of their fief as well. However, they weren't without their own problems. Since her parents had eloped, there were still ill feelings between her father and grandparents; her Uncle Reginald wound up disowning the family.

A family as distinguished as the Earl of Bancroft's had even more bonds. The burden of the role they had to fulfill was heavy, and the masses often came to them. One could not safeguard their house and fief with kindness alone; there were many family heads who spared little thought for their families, often citing an abundance of work as an excuse for not spending time with them.

Fiona let those thoughts wash away and said in a deliberately cheerful voice, "It's nice, isn't it? Although it's the reason I'm on the verge of being betrothed against my will."

"That's true. The grass is always greener, I suppose."

Her father was trying to get her married only because he loved her, after all. Fiona had no desire to go through with it, but she knew her father thought of her happiness.

"We'll do the introductions again at a later date, when my father is in a calmer state. I would also like to introduce you to my sister."

"Your sister?"

"Didn't you see her this morning? She was with me in the hall."

"I'm sorry. I didn't."

He truly did seem like this was the first he was hearing of her sister. He must not have noticed her. Perhaps he had been distracted by her father making such a fuss, but Cecilia had been standing right next to her, worried for her condition.

It couldn't be that his aversion to women is so strong that he just naturally blocks out their very presence from his vision, right? She was thinking about how serious his condition truly was, if that were the case, as the carriage pulled up to her house. They stopped at the same spot from which they had departed, and Giles elegantly helped her step down.

Having heard the sounds of the carriage, Hans opened the front door to reveal her anxious-looking father. For some reason, he held a large cushion. He must have been pacing back and forth, unable to regain his composure; having anticipated as much, Fiona couldn't help but smile crookedly.

However, he was with someone she had not been expecting. "Norman?"

Next to her father stood Norman. There was a bit of distance between Fiona and the doorway, but she could tell there was a hint of surprise in his usual smile.

At the sound of her voice, Giles followed her gaze, assessing Norman's appearance. "The aforementioned childhood friend?"

"Yes. But they told me he wouldn't be here until the weekend."

That morning Hans hadn't said anything about expecting

Norman. Of course, they didn't have such a formal relationship that he needed to give prior notice before arriving. He may have just been in the area and felt like dropping by.

Or...did my father call for him because of Lord Giles? Well, she would get to the bottom of it soon enough.

"Oh, I almost forgot—thank you so much for this outing. The park was beautiful, and I had a lovely time."

"Fiona." He was still holding her hand, which he had taken to help her step down. Instead of letting her go, he pulled her to him, closing the distance between them completely.

Huh?

She was snugly locked in his arms, just as she had been that night in the garden. His arms were firmly, and unyieldingly, wrapped around her waist. When Fiona looked up at Giles in surprise, his face blocked the blue sky from her sight. She blinked and the next thing she knew, his grayish-blue eyes were very close to hers and his sleek hair was tickling her forehead.

They were so close. Too close.

He stopped just close enough that their lips were nearly touching. From everyone else's angle at the front door, it probably did look like they were kissing.

Fiona was breathless with surprise. When Giles whispered, she felt the sensation of his breath against her skin before she heard his words: "Does this make you uncomfortable?"

"No—" *I don't dislike this, b-but why?!*

"Hopefully that will be enough for the baron to think we're in love."

Fiona understood then. Since he was unable to properly introduce himself that morning, he decided to put on a show instead.

Just as they had discovered with Hans, actions were far more convincing than words. Still, there was such a thing as crossing the line, especially when he did things that caught her off guard like this. *D-don't just take me by surprise like this!*

He could've at least warned her. Her head and heart were both so shaken, however, that she couldn't get any words out. Satisfied by how she went along with it, Giles finally let her go. He bowed with a radiant smile to the petrified men at the front door before climbing back into the carriage.

Before he left, Giles told her he would see her the next day. Fiona watched him go, finally cognizant of the heat in her cheeks. It was then that, behind her, she heard something large toppling to the ground.

He must be finding all this oh-so amusing! Fiona knew he disliked women, yet he performed the act convincingly.

Now that they had promised to be truthful to one another and not do anything that would make them uncomfortable, he must have decided that he no longer needed to act the perfect son of an earl. Certain behaviors were necessary for their act, and she didn't mind him touching her so familiarly, but now she was certain that the Icy Scion had a penchant for mischief: every time Giles caught her unaware, there was a glint of amusement in his grayish-blue eyes.

From the way he spoke in the palace garden, she sensed that he had built up a great resentment for society—particularly the opposite sex. It was possible that he had acted mischievously in order to let off steam.

Fiona was still thinking about how complex Giles really was, as her family and friend gathered around the table for a late lunch.

In a timid voice, Cecilia asked, "Um, Sister? Was that man just now your—"

A loud, hacking cough cut her off: their father was choking on his food.

"Oh my! Are you all right?" Norman, who sat next to him, rubbed his back to help him recover. Their father's eyes still looked teary with pain as he accepted a glass of water from Hans.

"Please, get ahold of yourself, my lord. Otherwise, I shall begin to worry for the future."

"Th-there is no—" Their father coughed again.

Because he had a head start in dealing with this new situation, Hans was perfectly collected as he tried to pacify Fiona's father. While he served the Clayburns, his chief loyalty was to Fiona and Cecilia. Proof of that was in the fact that he always took the girls' sides when they got into a dispute with their father. Even now, he turned a blind eye to Giles's earlier "misconduct."

"I can't believe Fiona has a beau." Norman's carefree statement incited yet another round of coughing from the baron. It really did seem like all that Norman felt about the situation was surprise. This made it clearer than ever to Fiona that Norman had no special feelings for her, especially given that he knew of their fathers' plan for them. "I'm especially surprised that it's Lord Lowell, of all people, though. How long have you two known each other?"

"We met the other night at the party for the prince. At the palace."

"Wow! That's so recent. I had no idea."

Neither did Fiona. How could she have known three days ago that all these events would unfold?

Fiona set down her silverware and looked around the table, starting with her father, who was finally breathing normally again. "I hadn't intended to keep it a secret from you all. Even I feel this is all happening very fast... I'm sorry if I worried you."

Her downcast eyes prompted Cecilia to say, "B-but, Sister, we're all just surprised. None of us are angry."

"That's right, Fiona. I was a bit worried that you had gotten in over your head after hearing that you're seeing such a big shot, but seeing what happened earlier, it seems like he's more infatuated with you than the other way around."

"D-do you think so?"

Norman exchanged a look with Cecilia and nodded. "Yeah."

Does that mean then that Giles is doing a better job at acting the part than I am? Even though neither of us has any dating experience. That was a little annoying. She would have to do better to properly act the role of a girl in love.

Still, to be fair, Giles did have Lord Russel to turn to. Fiona could ask Olga for advice, but she wasn't confident that she could skillfully keep the plan a secret while discussing romantic matters with her best friend.

That meant that she could only rely on novels. Nevertheless... *I shall not lose to him!* She was strangely invigorated by the thought of this competition.

"But I had no idea he was like that. I guess the rumor about him being the Icy Scion wasn't so accurate after all."

"Argh!" The baron clutched at his chest as he recalled the spectacle he had just witnessed.

It turned out that Cecilia was the one who gave him the cushion, insisting he needed something to keep his hands occupied. It was a good thing she had given it to him too, since it prevented him from hitting his head when he fell.

The baron made some kind of swallowing noise in his throat before he finally said, "A-anyway, Fiona. Once we are done with our meal, I would like you to come to my room."

"Yes, Father." Fiona nodded obediently, even as her shoulders drooped and a pain pricked at her chest.

An hour later, her father at last recognized her relationship with Giles.

CHAPTER 7

Playing the Part of His Lover

AS GILES LEFT the castle's assembly hall, several people rushed after him.

"Lord Lowell, are you free to discuss this further?"

"I'm sorry, but I have a previous engagement I must attend to. We'll speak another time," Giles said, heading outside. He wasn't late for his date, but he felt impatient when he imagined Fiona waiting for him.

Giles gave a sidelong glance at the line of carriages at the entrance waiting for their masters' return. He exited through the castle gates to find his own carriage waiting for him, just as instructed.

"Welcome back, my lord." With the driver's greeting as the cue, the footman set down a small stepladder just in time for Giles's arrival.

"Were you waiting long?"

"Not at all. About fifteen minutes, perhaps."

The timing wasn't perfect, but it was thanks to Giles's skill as the day's acting chairman that parliament ended roughly on time. It normally ran late.

He had foisted the wrap-up duties onto Richard, but he couldn't shake the feeling that Richard, amused as he was by Giles's plans, was the one to drive him out. He was certain that Richard would show up later that night to hound him for details.

Giles opened the box-shaped landau doors of the carriage to find his beloved—or rather, the woman playing the part of his beloved—waiting inside.

She looked up, surprised, from her novel. "Oh, good afternoon. You're here sooner than I expected."

"Am I?"

Given the book she had with her, it seemed she expected to be left waiting longer. She must've been aware of parliament's tendency to run late. Most daughters only knew enough about their father's occupation to say what it was, but Fiona must've talked to her father about it in depth.

"I warned the shop, so you didn't have to rush."

"I just urged some of the more verbose members to hurry up a bit, that's all."

"Really? That's all?"

"It's the truth," Giles said, taking the seat across from her. "By the way, why are you sitting all the way over there?"

Fiona was tucked in the corner of the four-person carriage, making herself small, perhaps so as not to be seen. She closed her book, and her eyes darted about uncomfortably.

Did something happen? Many family members of viscounts and barons served the Bancrofts. It was possible that some would adopt an arrogant attitude toward lower-ranking nobles and the gentry, because of whom they worked for.

Giles had gone out of his way to personally select the servants he brought with him to welcome this woman from an obscure baron's family, but if something had happened, then he needed to settle her fears at once. As the carriage began moving, he asked, "Were my servants discourteous toward you?"

"Hmm? Oh, no, not at all. It was very kind of them to come all the way to my home to pick me up. No, that's not the reason I'm sitting over here." Fiona met his gaze and offered him a crooked smile. "It's only that it's my first time riding in such an impressive carriage. I'm not used to sitting in one this big."

"I see." Giles was relieved by her simple response.

Not only were the interior and exterior of this carriage decorated but so were the suspension and other fittings. It certainly was impressive and comfortable to ride in. It was crafted to his father's tastes and for his practical use—the Earl of Bancroft traveled a great deal—but it was extravagant, even for a noble.

House Bancroft's carriages were all made similarly, regardless of their type. Fiona would simply have to get used to it. "It's hard to talk when you're hiding in the corner like that."

"I'm sorry." At his encouragement, Fiona nervously slid over to sit near the center of the bench.

Her halting movements reminded Giles of a squirrel he had once seen at the hunting grounds. It was so different from her usual, captivating elegance that he felt himself on the verge of smiling.

Perhaps it would be best to fill the space, then, if she felt it too empty. "I'll have cushions put in here next time."

"Oh, you needn't go so far for my sake... Wait, next time?" A faraway look appeared in Fiona's eye, as though she wondered whether there would be a next time. However, this ruse of theirs had only just begun, and it would last until the end of the social season. Of course, there would be a next time, and another after that.

She's sharp, but sometimes she doesn't see the forest for the trees. It was hard to believe that this was the same dignified woman who stood so defiantly in front of the art dealer, Gordon, in Giles's parlor. And yet, he didn't find this dualistic nature of hers—so different from the other women he had known—disagreeable.

Fiona must've told the driver their destination before Giles arrived. He parted the curtain slightly, confirming that they were heading into the center of town. "By the way, who is this dressmaker you know?"

"It's a shop called Maison de Michele. They don't make men's clothing, so perhaps you've never heard of it. One of my regular customers at the art gallery runs it as a hobby." Fiona described it as a hideaway, tucked away down an alley off the main street. It was run by the owner and her designer—both of whom came from the same neighboring nation—and two seamstresses.

"Like a hideaway? I think my sister has mentioned such a shop before."

"Has she really? The owner will be happy to hear that even the marchioness knows of her shop."

Fiona sounded happy, as if she were the one being praised. But in fact, Giles's sister had lamented to him that she couldn't get an appointment with the shop. She described a wait of a year or more to have a gown made that could be worn to functions at the castle.

This was probably the most popular dress shop in all the capital. "Did you get that dress you're wearing today there?"

The pale-colored dress Fiona wore was considerably modest. Nothing Giles had seen her wear felt drab, but it didn't look like something made by a famous dressmaker either.

Despite the rudeness of his question, Fiona chuckled, as if he had just made a joke. "Of course not. I've never had a dress tailored here in the capital."

"Really?" It would hardly be unusual if she had. Giles's mother and sister were always finding excuses to have new dresses made, and they would summon jewelers too. He assumed that was ordinary for any noble woman to do.

"It's not that I have no interest in fashion, but I rarely go to parties and a good portion of our customers at the gallery are commoners. I've simply never had an opportunity to wear a pretty dress. Back at our fief, I often ride horseback through the woods and help out with the farmwork."

Giles found these to be reasonable explanations for putting off buying new clothes and accessories for so long. He had no particular interest in or taste for women's clothing, but he thought that Fiona would look much prettier if she dressed differently.

Fiona continued, "Mrs. Bennett always tells me I need to dress up a bit more."

"My sister is that type as well. Wait, Mrs. Bennett? What's her full name?"

"Huh? Oh, it's Mrs. Chloe Marianne Michele Bennett."

Wasn't that the name of the founder of the Bennett Trading Company—a prominent company even in their country?

Fiona likely wouldn't know it since she didn't spend much time immersing herself in society, but Mrs. Bennett was even more shrewd than the late Mr. Bennett. She was famous among Giles's grandfather's generation as a key figure behind the scenes of Bennett Trading Company.

Furthermore, when he asked how long ago Fiona had made her appointment, she told him casually that she had made it two days prior. Mrs. Bennett, she explained, was always inviting Fiona to her shop when she visited the gallery, and Fiona had finally accepted.

Giles had no doubt that Miranda would be green with envy if she heard this.

"She's always offering to make something for me. To be honest, I planned to go there just to chat today, but perhaps this would be a perfect opportunity..."

The letter of introduction Fiona had brought with her to the Bancrofts' estate was from Lord Talbott, the former prime minister himself. And now she mentioned knowing a powerful figure from the business world. Moreover, the way Fiona had dropped the name of the Academy's chief examiner to Gordon made it sound like she knew him personally.

There was no way that Baron Clayburn had such connections. Giles surmised that these were connections Fiona herself had forged while working at the gallery, but these were all prominent people that he wouldn't expect a mere daughter of a baron to know.

"You're—how do I put it?—very well-connected."

"I would hardly say that." From the astonished look she gave him, he guessed she didn't realize the gravity of her personal connections. She sunk into thought for a moment, then abruptly smiled. "But I am blessed. All the people I've come to know are so kind."

That's what she thinks?

It was normal in the life of a noble to use and be used by others. One's connections and bonds became a source of strength. With that many connections, she surely could have found a way to avoid her engagement. For example, she could have asked Mrs. Bennett to recommend her for a government-financed scholarship, giving Fiona an in to the woman's homeland as a student. Fiona had enough knowledge and aesthetic sense to stonewall someone like Gordon. She could have even used her connections at the academy if she wanted to further immerse herself in the art world. Giles could come up with a multitude of ways she could've impeded her father's plan.

In other words, she didn't need to pretend to be Giles's beloved. But it seemed she hadn't even realized that she could use her acquaintances to serve her own ends. *Lord Talbott and shrewd businesspeople do not so easily accept others into their good graces.*

She probably doesn't realize that either, judging from what she's said.

"Did you meet Lord Talbott at your gallery too?"

"Oh, yes, that's right... However, I know him not as Lord Talbott, the prime minister, but Uncle Talbott, the head of his house." Fiona was unusually evasive about the subject, stressing that he was someone she knew from her private life. She brought a finger to her lips, smiling as if to say she couldn't tell him anymore. "It's a secret. It's not a lie, so you'll have to pardon me. After all, I didn't pry into how exactly you managed to end parliament on time."

"Very well, then," Giles agreed reluctantly. He didn't pry further.

Was she free of ambition or just oblivious? Unfortunately, she lacked the right disposition for a noble. Perhaps it was because she had no ulterior motives that Giles was inclined to go along with this silly ruse of theirs. But of course, the whole thing had turned out to be not as bad as he had feared.

He couldn't get enough of her constantly changing expressions and her fearless, forthright responses. And best of all, no unpleasant feelings welled up when he had to touch her, even when all he was doing was escorting her. It must've been because she showed no sign of intent to seduce him.

But I wasn't expecting her to be so shocked by that. He had kissed her cheek farewell on a whim, trying to imitate Richard. Fiona had frozen up, but her slender shoulders and cheek had felt so warm and soft.

Perhaps it was because she wore a thin corset. Among all the women he had been forced to dance with at parties, he had never felt such warmth. It made him keenly aware that she was another human being, which certainly helped. That felt true the previous day as well. It was fascinating how, every time he closed the physical distance between them, her amber-colored eyes opened wide, as if she were frozen in time.

And when he saw Norman at the Clayburn's residence, new feelings welled up inside him. His body had moved of its own accord; he had no idea what the impetus for that had been.

"By the way," Fiona's voice interrupted his reverie. She sat up straight and let out a short breath as she began to speak of the very events Giles had been thinking about. "My father now recognizes our relationship, thanks to what you did yesterday. For now, I think we should wait and see how things go."

"What do you mean 'for now'?"

She explained that Norman was at her home yesterday because her father summoned him to discuss the future, out of his fears about Fiona and Giles's relationship. "Naturally, he's still keeping the engagement a secret from me, so I asked Norman in confidence to tell me what he said." Baron Hayes had even been included in Baron Clayburn and Norman's discussion the night before; Fiona could only give a chagrinned smile at being left out of the conversation. "We're still going to hold the party at our home next weekend as planned, but they decided to hold off on announcing our engagement."

Giles's improvisation had worked. Giles was of a higher rank than the Clayburns in terms of both pedigree and peerage. Baron Clayburn had no choice but to acquiesce when the son of an earl came to call for his daughter, and he certainly couldn't announce that she was engaged to another man.

"You have been a great help to me. Thank you."

"That's one goal achieved, then."

"Yes. However, they're not going to cancel any prospect of engagement altogether."

"I see." It seemed that Baron Clayburn and the others believed their courtship would be short-lived.

Most parents would fall all over themselves at the chance to marry their daughter off to someone of a higher rank, but it seemed Baron Clayburn was the opposite. It was evident he would wait for them to break up and then try to have Fiona wed Norman once things cooled down.

"I can understand why he doesn't think things will work out between us," Fiona said. "Fortunately, he doesn't realize that this is all an act, so he's deluding himself for the moment."

Giles could understand why Baron Clayburn thought as much—but did he have such a low opinion of his daughter?

However, Fiona clearly understood and agreed with her father's reasoning. "I'm sure he's been planning for some time to not only announce our engagement but also announce Norman as his heir. I feel bad that the succession announcement will be delayed for Norman too."

Though Giles thought it must be uncomfortable that their future breakup was a condition for that, Fiona had a sunny expression on her face. She said she would be content as long as they managed to buy her more time. She said cheerfully that

PLAYING THE PART OF HIS LOVER

she had written to her uncle for advice and that his response had at last arrived. "Uncle promised that he is my ally in this matter. Although nothing has been decided for sure, that alone is reassuring to me."

"I see."

Fiona had to do her best to make arrangements before the end of their contract and their eventual breakup. However, there was a possibility that the rumors about them might circulate out of their control and hurt her reputation. Giles would be partially responsible if that happened, whether he liked it or not.

The thought was oddly depressing.

"And, well, it's...because of what you did that made Father ultimately decide to postpone the engagement," Fiona said in an unusually halting manner, which gave Giles a good idea of what she was referring to. She averted her gaze for a moment. When she looked at him again, she said with determination, "Could you please warn me from now on?"

"Warn you?"

"I am unaccustomed to these sorts of things. Each time you have done something like that, I was so shocked that I was unable to respond as one's beloved might. It simply won't do."

Giles, who had braced himself for protests about his behavior, felt the tension leave his shoulders. *In other words, she doesn't dislike it when I do that.*

He had no intention of forcing her to endure something she didn't like, but it was pointless to act that way if his actions had no effect. And what he did was highly effective.

As long as Fiona didn't say no, then that much wouldn't change. "I was acting on the spur of the moment, so I don't think I could give you a warning. And it would be unnatural for me to stop and warn you every single time."

Fiona must have known that. She flinched minutely. "B-but then—"

"You know what I'm trying to say. Okay, how about this?" Before she could say anything else, Giles moved across from his seat and sat down next to Fiona. The bench had more than enough room for two adults to sit side by side, but Giles deliberately sat close enough for their shoulders to touch.

Fiona twisted away from him, astonished. "Huh? What are you—?"

"Isn't it obvious? We're going to have to make it so you don't startle whenever I touch you without warning."

Fiona blinked rapidly, wide-eyed, trying to comprehend what he meant. She looked like a cat who had frozen at a loud noise.

Giles lifted one of her hands. "Like this." He placed his hand in her palm, moving her hand up and down to the movements of the carriage in a soothing motion. Gradually, Fiona relaxed.

But then she looked at him anxiously. "And you're okay with this?"

"I'm fine. If you aren't, I'll stop." She peered deep into his eyes again, then suddenly dropped her gaze. "Fiona?"

After a pause, she said resolutely, "Very well then." She laced her slender fingers with his.

Fiona looked up at him, a daring glint in her amber eyes.

PLAYING THE PART OF HIS LOVER

With her other hand, she reached to stroke his dark blond fringe. Her hand stopped just above his ear.

He looked at her in surprise.

"You ran to the carriage, didn't you?" she said.

His hair must have been in a state of disarray. There was nothing alluring in her touch—she acted as if he were family. He could sense her genuine concern for his appearance and felt no discomfort.

She's so different. From Giles himself. From his family.

She didn't behave like the she wanted to take something from him. He breathed deeply; instead of his body growing cold, he felt warm relief spread through his heart.

Fiona touched him again to fix his hair before nodding to herself with satisfaction. She grasped his other hand and then pressed her lips together. "I shall not lose to you. I'm going to do my best to act as your beloved, so I hope you're ready."

When had this turned into a competition? She really was something else. Giles felt bad, because she wore such a serious expression, but he nearly burst out laughing. But another part of him was glad that it was Fiona who played the part of his beloved. "I accept your challenge."

"Oh, but do tell me if I ever overstep," she added hastily. "The last thing I would want to do is bite the hand that feeds me, so to speak." It seemed she already had forgotten about their competition.

Giles tried to stop himself from laughing again, but this time he couldn't help but let a brief chuckle slip out.

As expected, Richard came calling in the dead of night. Before he even sat down, he asked, "So, how's it going?"

"Hello to you too." Giles laughed dryly. He had already cleared the room, but he double-checked that no one was listening outside the door before saying, "Pretty good...I think."

"You think? You don't need to be modest. I'm already starting to hear rumors about your romantic affairs."

"That was fast."

"That's rumor for you."

Giles asked what kind of rumors Richard had heard, and it turned out to be eyewitness testimonies from the park. it had only been a day, but that was more than enough time for news to spread. Giles was both surprised and impressed.

When he recounted the trip to Mrs. Bennett's shop, Richard listened intently. "You went to Maison de Michele? You've got to be kidding me."

"Fiona only intended to drop by her friend's place, for tea or some such thing."

"Did she, now? This lady just continues to surprise us, doesn't she?"

He was right. Fiona had spoken in a foreign language the entire time they were at the shop. Fiona claimed she had "only studied a bit," but she surprised Giles by conversing at length. Although Giles understood the gist of their conversation, they spoke of clothes and art, using so many technical terms that there were gaps in his comprehension.

Moreover, Mrs. Bennett, the designer, and the seamstresses surrounded Fiona while completely ignoring Giles. It was refreshing to melt into the background and peacefully observe their excited chatter.

"So I'm guessing she had a dress made?"

"The designer and Mrs. Bennett were more excited about it than Fiona. Unsurprisingly, though, it won't be ready for this weekend."

That meant that Fiona's commissioned dress wouldn't be ready for the Earl of Burleigh's ball. The shop had some dresses Fiona liked that could be worn after some minor alternations, but everyone else decided that if she was to wear one of their designs, it would be one made just for her.

"Yeah, that probably is for the best. It'll be most impactful if she changes her image after it's already well-known that you two are together."

"Not that she'd become some kind of spectacle," Giles put in after a pause.

"What's that now?"

"I think how she dresses now is fine."

"Is that so?" Richard grinned suggestively, earning himself a glare. Raising his hands, he said, "But if she has acquaintances at such a big shop, then why does she always wear such modest clothing?"

"Ah, that? She said they belonged to her late mother."

Baron Clayburn had several dresses he had personally selected for Fiona's mother. Fiona had made a few alterations so that she could wear them herself. There were no decorations on the back or sides of the dresses; that way her mother could lie down easily in them. The fabric was light and lacked layers, so she would not be exhausted by the weight. Their colors were easy on the eyes, and they were designed to not burden the body. They had been made in the hope that Fiona's mother would wear them after her recovery. Sadly, she never had the chance to wear them all.

Fiona's sister spent much of her time confined to bed, just like their mother, so the dresses came in handy for her. Fiona wore them too, for her father and for her grandparents when they visited. That was how Fiona and her sister had repurposed the clothes they inherited from their late mother.

Mrs. Bennett told Giles all this while Fiona was in the changing room; Fiona hadn't told her not to. "And because of her situation, I cannot possibly impose myself on her," she said. "The fact is that her clothes are of high-quality fabric and tailoring. However, to be completely honest with you, the color and design of her clothes do no justice to her complexion or hair." Mrs. Bennett was pleased indeed that Fiona had finally granted her permission to make her some clothes that would suit her well.

The extraordinary businesswoman looked at Giles with a gaze as calm as a lake in winter. He was used to such appraising stares, but he felt like she was looking at him with a different kind of zeal in her eye. "Lord Lowell, I shall withhold passing judgment on what kind of man you must be, but for now you have earned my approval for inspiring her to renovate her wardrobe."

Giles couldn't help responding with a crooked smile. She spoke to him like she was Fiona's grandmother, but he didn't mind it at all. Everyone but Fiona was thrilled, and with accessories included, she wound up ordering far more than she had originally intended.

Fiona was angry that Giles took care of the payment without asking her first, but he managed to talk her into it by saying it was a necessary expense—especially since she wouldn't need such fineries if it weren't for Giles.

"Ah, I see," Richard said. "And of course, you'll be seeing her tomorrow, right?"

"I have work in the morning, so I'll see her tomorrow afternoon."

"All right. I'll go ahead and get you a reservation at a tearoom that's popular among women. We don't have many days left before the weekend, so you need to go show off during your walk around the capital— Hey, don't look so annoyed by this!"

Giles's annoyance was not about seeing Fiona again but because he had to do so under the troublesome pretext of fueling more rumors. "At least, that's how I feel. By the way—"

"I know what you're going to ask. Otto Gordon has decided to delay the opening of his art gallery on Low Street." Richard was able to intuit his question at a glance. It was handy having trusted friends in times like this. "I bumped into one of his employees cleaning up and asked them about it. Gordon hadn't said when they would open, but he apparently left to buy plenty of new paintings and plans to open officially when he returns."

"Do you really think he'll be back?"

"I think it's fifty-fifty."

They were unable to ascertain whether it had been an accident or intentional, but the fact of the matter was that he had tried to sell a fake painting to the Marchioness of Colet. She hadn't suffered any damages since she refused to purchase it, and his sister wouldn't take Gordon to court because she detested bad publicity. However, the marchioness and her family were sure to keep a watchful eye on Gordon's movements and warn their close friends about him.

This is why they assumed Gordon wouldn't make any sudden moves. However...

"Members of House Brook and Fowler have bought new works from famous painters that have not yet been made public," said Richard.

"They did? What about your family?"

"He came to my family's estate as well to try to sell to us. He also went to House Garland."

Each of the houses Richard mentioned belonged to the same circle as those of the Marquis of Colet and the Earl of Bancroft. It was hard to call this a coincidence.

"I couldn't tell if the paintings they had in the gallery were real or not."

"I see. I hate to ask, but could you keep an eye on them for a bit longer?"

"You sure are keeping me busy."

"Sorry," Giles said, a perfunctory reply to the slight protest. Richard responded with an accepting smile.

"Ha ha. What I mean is that this is all kinds of fun. The social season's never been so interesting. And this is all thanks to Miss Clayburn."

With a wave of his hand, Richard made his way out. Pensively, Giles took out letter paper and an envelope and picked up a pen. On the face of the envelope, he wrote to Gallery Roche—the art gallery at which Fiona worked.

TRUE LOVE Fades Away When the Contract Ends

One Star in the Night Sky

CHAPTER 8

Now, to the Party

FIONA RELEASED A LONG BREATH as she gazed at the ring on her left ring finger.

The surface of the golden hoop was smooth. Its center stone was a large, canary yellow diamond matching Fiona's amber eyes, and on either side of that center stone sat a clear diamond. Fiona's slender finger was completely hidden beneath the three gems.

The ring, which glimmered in both afternoon sunlight and the lamplight of early evening, was a gift from Giles. The other day, they had visited the tearoom Richard had recommended, which was located down a narrow lane that carriages could not pass through. They both enjoyed the presentation and the flavor of the food. Unexpectedly, Giles took Fiona to a boutique on the return trip. The next thing she knew, she was walking out of the shop with this ring on her finger.

The boutique was that of a long-established designer brand. The first ring they were shown was made of thick platinum, with a cluster of white diamonds arranged in the shape of a flower.

Fiona stared at it in wonder, but it wasn't to Giles's liking. He asked something of the proprietor, and the second ring brought out was the one now adorning Fiona's finger.

Giles held it up next to Fiona's face, looking between the ring and her eyes to compare the colors. The ring also happened to fit her perfectly; so he nodded, satisfied, and they walked out of the shop with it still upon Fiona's finger.

She had somehow managed to endure the whole endeavor while they were in public, but as soon as she got into the carriage, she started questioning Giles about the ring. Giles, however, merely shrugged off her questions.

He had already claimed that the cost of the dresses and accessories were "necessary expenses" and insisted on paying for them. And here he was again, buying her expensive things. It would not do. But Giles replied, handsome and nonchalant, "This is meant as a substitute for the contract."

"What?"

"You can use that as collateral in the event that I don't perform to your expectations."

In other words, Giles gave the ring to Fiona so that she would have it if he broke their agreement. Meanwhile, if Fiona were to violate the agreement, she would pay Giles the cost of the ring. It was a substitute for the contract, as the two of them had agreed. "Because you were worried about not having a contract, right?"

"Uh, yes, I suppose I was." Having received this explanation, Fiona found herself with no grounds for further objection.

She had heard that the Earl of Bancroft's family had an heirloom ring that was passed down to the spouse of the heir. When Fiona still displayed some reluctance about the ring, Giles told her that if she simply couldn't accept it, then she should bring it back to the boutique, which finally made her surrender.

All he had done was draw from his experiences as someone who grew up surrounded by aristocratic schemes and politicking. Persuading a country-bred woman like Fiona must have felt easier than taking candy from a baby. *Though I still think he went overboard with this one.*

Fiona did understand that wearing a ring he gave her would be an effective way of showing off their relationship, but this was the kind of ring you would give a woman you actually intended to marry. Giles insisted that this level of opulence was normal for his family, but it certainly wasn't for Fiona's.

Besides, looking at the ring and wearing it were completely different matters. Fiona had been too afraid to ask how much it cost, but she broke out in a cold sweat just thinking about having such an expensive ring in her possession for the duration of their charade. *I still feel nervous, even now.*

Normally, Fiona only wore a single brooch; she had never worn a ring before. The weight of it on her finger and the way the stone glimmered made her anxious. She sighed over her situation for the umpteenth time, when there was a knock at her bedroom door.

"Miss Fiona, Lord Lowell is here to see you."

"Thank you, Hans. I'll be right down."

That night was, at last, the night of the ball at the Earl of Burleigh's estate. Whether she liked it or not, the ring was here to stay, and now it was time to step out her door and onto the stage.

She looked down at the sparkly ring and took a deep breath. *If this is my lot, then I will have to do my best to make sure everyone notices the ring!* Fiona calmed her mind and stepped through the door.

Giles spotted the ring as she descended the stairs. He scooped up her left hand and brought the tips of her fingers to his lips. "It looks stunning on you."

"Thank you. I think it's a bit too lavish for someone like me, though."

"Nonsense."

Lord Russel's coaching has been tremendous. Lord Giles has become the perfect gentleman, from his actions to his words.

Fiona caught a glimpse of her father, who looked on the verge of fainting again, and quickly reclaimed her hand.

Giles smiled knowingly as he turned to face her father. "Baron Clayburn, while we may be a bit late in our return this evening, rest assured that I shall see your daughter home safely."

"I'll see you later, Father."

"Y-yes. Have a good time, Fiona. And L-L-L-Lord Lowell, I trust my daughter is in good hands."

Fiona gave her father a reassuring nod, but he continued to act as strangely as ever. She exchanged looks with Hans and Cecilia, who both stood behind him, and then left.

It was the time of year when the days were long, so it was still bright outside as they headed to the evening's party. Fiona greeted the driver and footman, both of whom she was now well-acquainted with, and stepped into the carriage. Giles sat down next to her as if it were the most natural thing in the world.

"Thank you for the flowers yesterday. Mr. Roche was very pleased by them."

"I'm glad to hear that."

Given how busy Giles was, the only day he had been available to go out with Fiona that week was the day before. Because they couldn't see one another, he sent a bouquet of flowers to the gallery. While Richard's advice was unimpeachable, Giles was really pushing the limit.

Touching him and being touched by him... Holding hands and quick pecks on the cheek when parting were all still at the heart of it, and now, with repeated exposure over such a short span of time, Fiona had stopped freezing up. His touches still made her heart skip a beat, but she was able to keep calm.

Unlike Fiona, Giles had always been adept at behaving as her beau, but she thought even he was becoming more natural at it with practice. At this point, his behavior made it hard to believe that he was uncomfortable around women.

I'm starting to think that the day when he loses the title of Icy Scion and becomes known as Lord Russel the Second is not too far off. Is he really okay with all this?

The carriage began to move. Fiona thought her impolite thoughts about Giles and Richard, as she retrieved a golden pocket watch from the pocket of her dress.

"Lord Giles, I would like you to have this."

"A watch?" Giles looked closely at the pocket watch. He clicked the lid open to find clean-cut hands marking the passage of time on the watch's white face.

"Both parties must make an exchange in a contract. It is pointless for me to be the only one to receive something. However, I doubt that watch is comparable to what you've given to me," Fiona explained, lifting her hand to indicate the ring. "My family possesses few pieces of jewelry. This is the first thing I bought with the money I earned. It represents the first time I ever picked something out for myself."

All their jewelry and other valuables had been sold to pay for her mother's and Cecilia's medical expenses. Fiona learned this when she prepared for her debut into high society, but she felt no hint of reproach toward her father. For one thing, Fiona had no interest in dressing up. She had considered having new things prepared for Cecilia's coming-of-age, but the items their grandmother was willing to lend them would do. That meant that the only two things in Fiona's possession that were worthy of being used for their contract were the painting of the common redpoll or this pocket watch.

The painting was hanging back at their estate in their fief, not here in their townhouse in the capital. That left the pocket watch as the only thing she had to offer.

"I found it at an auction that I visited for work." To be exact, she had accompanied Mr. Roche, the gallery's owner, to a painting auction where she noticed the watch. It hadn't been on exhibit but was instead among various other goods someone in their trade had picked up on their way home from purchasing paintings.

"So it's an antique, then."

"That's right. I don't know much about antiques, but I couldn't take my eyes off it."

The face of the watch was faded, and the fine hands showed signs of rust. It had no engravings or markings to tell the time at a glance, but intricate arabesque patterns were engraved on the lid, drawing the eye to their shape. It didn't weigh much either, so once she picked it up, she didn't want to let it go.

Because the seller was an acquaintance, she convinced him to knock the price down considerably, but it had still cost a great deal for her. Nevertheless, it was hers.

"This must mean a lot to you then."

"I'm attached to it, yes."

Giles looked like he wanted to say something, but this item was her part of their agreement. She couldn't give him just any trivial thing.

"I had it repaired, so it is usable. There is a skilled craftsman who lives on our land."

He was a taciturn, stubborn, narrow-minded, and scary-looking clockmaker with no apprentice to speak of. But he was, beyond any doubt, skilled in his trade. When Fiona made the request, he polished the watch and spent a great deal of time repairing it for her. Once he cleaned it, even the smallest scratches shone beautifully. Fortunately, it hadn't been missing any parts, and she was pleased to learn that he had even repaired the minute repeater.

Fiona took the watch back from Giles to show him that it could announce the time with a pleasant dinging sound. The sound of small chimes filled the carriage like falling stars, drowning out the sounds of the axles. "I know this is of nowhere near equivalent value to the ring," she said, "but it would bring me peace of mind if you would hold on to it for now."

"Very well, then. I shall." Giles took out a silk handkerchief and carefully wrapped the watch in it before slipping it into his jacket's inner pocket.

Y-you don't have to be that careful with it!

Even if it was valuable to Fiona and one of her favorite things, surely Giles was used to handling objects of much finer quality than the watch. Something about his behavior embarrassed her, but it did make her happy to see her watch treated with such respect.

Not long thereafter, the carriage arrived at the Burleigh estate. Fiona sensed countless eyes fixed on her from the moment she stepped out of the carriage at the estate's front entrance.

This was likely the fruits of their efforts to get the rumor mill turning in their favor. She felt a pressure unmatched by any she had felt during their previous outings. "I had no idea people's gazes had such power."

She could sense, all at once, astonishment, curiosity, and burning jealousy from the way those eyes looked at her. She nearly faltered in spite of herself, but because she had Giles by her side, she managed to boldly face them. She held her head high, full of determination and a sense of responsibility to play her role.

Fiona had a feeling that women must always be fixated on Giles, given his social standing and good looks. She could hardly believe that he stood so unruffled in the face of so many people's stares.

"Fiona?"

"I'm fine. Just a little nervous."

They stared not at Fiona herself but at Giles Bancroft's beloved. She tried to convince herself of this, but perhaps her smile was unconvincing. Her fingertips on his arm tensed up unnaturally.

Giles touched her cheek, making it so she didn't have the presence of mind to notice the voices swelling up around them. His hand slid back behind her ear, and he bent down to quietly murmur, "You don't need to pay attention to our surroundings. And don't worry. I'll be here by your side the whole time."

"A-all right."

Likely, he made his voice as quiet as possible so that no one would overhear and realize it was all an act. That was why they usually spoke in close proximity. Although it was unkind on her heart, the familiar closeness brought her comfort.

His words commanding her to look only at him sounded arrogant, but he had reminded her again and again that their goal at this party was to flaunt their relationship and make sure that everyone knew they were together. In particular, they were to make Lady Caroline give up on Giles; socializing came second.

Be that as it may—

The next time I see Lord Russel, I'll have to ask him what kind of advice he's been giving Lord Giles!

As an expert on relations between the sexes, Richard's counsel was dependable, but Fiona feared what would happen if Giles's behavior escalated any further.

Fiona remembered Richard smiling astutely as they entered the hall. Lord and Lady Burleigh had arranged this ball to give their daughter a chance with Giles, since they were certain he would come alone. Their faces froze when they saw their plans wrecked so spectacularly. The host's daughter stood before them with her hair done up in beautiful ringlets, but Giles paid her no mind. He kept his hand firmly on Fiona's waist. As expected, this earned Fiona a sharp glare from Caroline.

Lord and Lady Burleigh tried to entreat him, but Giles skillfully navigated the conversation. Thanks to his talent with words, Fiona hadn't so much as a chance to speak before their audience with the party's hosts was over.

"Was that okay back there? I didn't do a thing." She had been breathtakingly nervous, but it felt far too simple to ask her to merely curtsy at them.

"Like I told you, I wasn't expecting you to do anything special."

"Yes, but—"

"I managed to get out of that without being invited to dance with her. You did great."

Contrary to Fiona's disappointment, Giles was pleased. His good mood radiated from his beautiful face amid their luxurious surroundings.

It seemed that, for most people, his bright smile was an unusual sight. As they proceeded through the crowded hall, Fiona was keenly aware of the many eyes that now followed not only her but Giles as well.

"Wow," Giles said, "I'm actually able to walk like normal with you by my side."

"I'm glad I could be of some use to you tonight." Hearing him speak so cheerfully helped her stop wallowing in how pathetic she felt and focus instead on his plight. Fiona had never thought of being able to simply walk in a straight line as something to be happy about. *Here I thought popularity was a good thing.*

The constant staring was already beginning to exhaust Fiona. She was willing to go along with things for the sake of the plan, but it might be bad for her health to push herself beyond her limits. She surveyed the venue and spotted a buffet that was a feast for the senses. He may have attended countless parties, but Fiona had a feeling that Giles never had the chance to savor the food that was served.

Since we're here, we might as well enjoy ourselves, right? It would be nice if he could feel a bit more at ease than usual, since she was there with him.

Thinking this, she looked up and met his gaze. They both smiled at one another, eliciting yet more commotion from their onlookers, but Fiona was determined to not pay them any mind.

The Earl of Burleigh's cook was renowned for his skill. Fiona was captivated by the sight of so many unusual hors d'oeuvres and desserts from which to choose, but before indulging, Giles first stopped a servant boy carrying a tray of drinks.

Worried that Fiona was thirsty from the stress, he asked, "Do you want something to drink?"

"Something without alcohol in it."

"Do you not drink?"

"Just in case." It wasn't as though Fiona abstained from drinking; she just didn't do it very often. Under her breath, she told him that she wouldn't want to drink too much and make an accidental slip. He nodded approvingly.

It seemed that, for the night, Giles had sealed away the somewhat curt side of him that Fiona had come to know. Part of that was likely because he was in a good mood, but he was also giving her alluring looks far more frequently than necessary. Fiona was amazed by his acting abilities.

Despite it all, she kept catching glimpses of genuine enjoyment in his expression. It was the same look he wore whenever he did something to make her freeze up, before he came up with an excuse for his behavior and seemed regretful over it.

I need to stay on my guard.

They'd started with a bang, but it wouldn't do to assume the whole night would go so smoothly. Even smiling back at Giles like she was in love took a considerable amount of effort. Nevertheless...

"No one's coming to speak with us," she murmured, as she accepted a cordial in a flute glass from Giles.

Fiona had braced herself to be swarmed by curious guests as soon as they stopped moving. However, people surrounded them only at a distance, watching. Fiona found it bewildering.

Of course, they didn't want people to ask them questions; it was better for them to not have to interact with a single person that night. She just hadn't expected to be neglected so completely by the other party guests.

"Fine with me," Giles said. "It would be more trouble to have them all prying into our affairs."

"True."

"Are you worried? Then we'll just have to put on a show so that they have no need to come to us with questions in the first place." Giles took her hand and boldly brought her fingers to his lips, showing off the ring on her finger. All the while, he gave her the mischievous expression she was on the lookout for.

Oh, he's done it again!

As anticipated, they heard muffled shrieks from the crowd—and then a familiar voice behind Fiona. "That's enough, you two lovebirds."

"Rick."

Richard made his entrance. Fiona had innumerable things to say to and ask him, but for the moment, she just sighed in relief.

As always, he was a stunning sight to behold. They garnered even more attention with the two most popular and eligible young men in high society assembled in one place. Fiona had the sense that they had entered the main act of the night's production.

"Good evening, Miss Clayburn." Fiona hadn't even noticed Richard taking her hand. She looked into his turquoise eyes as he smiled amiably at her.

Before she could so much as react, his lips were brushing against her fingers. She felt an intense sense of discomfort at the contact between her hand and his lips.

Why does it feel so different?

"Are you enjoying tonight's party?"

Richard released her hand before she could try to figure out her feelings "Y-yes, I am. Thank you."

And why did she feel relieved when Giles all but snatched her hand back?

Oh, I think I might know why. In the past week, she had grown accustomed to Giles's touch, but she hadn't known Richard's since seeing him in the parlor at the Bancroft estate. They were different people, so of course her reaction was different.

As she recollected herself, the cordial she had only had a sip of was taken from her hand—they were to go dance and show just how intimate they really were. The order came out of nowhere, but Richard's confident smile was persuasive.

"You've got to dance very closely to one another now to show how passionately in love you are," Richard whispered in hushed tones only the two of them could hear. He wore a satisfied smile on his face.

Fiona knew what she must do without being told. However, she wished he wouldn't incite Giles so.

Thanks to Richard, they waltzed perhaps a bit *too* close together—but as they did, she noticed Lady Caroline leaving the hall in a huff. *Good. It looks like I'm getting passing marks for my performance.* Fiona sighed, relieved that she had successfully played her part.

The song came to an end with one last grand spin. Suddenly, Richard stood right next to them. "Time to change partners. You'll have to deal with them a bit, unfortunately." He motioned with his thumb over his shoulder, indicating the crowd of curious onlookers.

"So be it." Giles glanced at them with disinterest as he reluctantly handed Fiona over to his friend.

Fiona was nothing but impressed with how well Giles acted the adoring beau. She knew she should act sad to leave his side, but she was out of breath from the dance and didn't have it in her.

Richard chuckled as Fiona's gaze followed Giles's exit from the dance ring. "Looks like things are going well between you two."

"Yes, thanks to all your help." She repositioned her hands with his and they began to dance. His lead was—unsurprisingly—flawless. Fortunately, the next song had a slower tempo, giving them a brief chance to talk. "Excuse me, Lord Russel, but I was wondering: Just what kind of advice have you been giving Lord Giles?"

"Hm?"

"I feel like he's been pushing the limits of his comfort."

"Has he now? How so?"

"H-how..." Her eyes darted about as she recalled examples. They were all a bit hard to convey in words.

Her hesitation made Richard grin. "If you can't give me any specific examples, then I won't be able to judge whether or not he really is pushing his boundaries."

Such impertinence!

His stiff delivery made her want to stop dancing and stamp her feet in frustration. It must've shown on her face because Richard smiled to sweeten her back up. "Ha ha, my apologies. In all seriousness, everything I've suggested has been pretty typical."

"Only typical things? Truly?"

"Of course. But you know, despite how he must seem, he's always had a caring heart. Why, I've often seen him taking care of the family's pet dog. Perhaps you've just drudged up that part of him again."

Did he just compare her to a dog?

And yet, it all made sense. "I see. So that's how he's been treating me."

"Wait, I didn't really mean for you to agree with that."

"No, it explains why he seeks so much physical contact between us."

"Are you really comparing yourself to a dog? No, no, what I said is wrong."

"Then perhaps he sees me more as a cat."

Richard burst out laughing, but it was the most apt comparison. At the very least, she was sure that Giles did not put her in the same category as most women. "Pfft... Ha ha... Well, putting that aside, until he was about ten years old, Giles was able to talk and conduct himself like any normal boy around girls. He even had a fiancée."

A fiancée. The word made Fiona blink. It had slipped her mind because she had only ever heard about how much he disliked women, but he was the heir of an earl. It was quite strange that he didn't already have a fiancée.

"But the engagement was canceled before any of us knew it, and his beloved dog died around the same time. He started distancing himself from people—or rather, from girls—ever since."

"I see." Ten years ago, Giles would have been younger than Cecilia was now. Fiona didn't know the particulars, but it must've come as such a shock to have so many bad things happen in quick succession at such a tender age.

As she twirled, she caught sight of Giles surrounded by a crowd. She thought their eyes met for a moment.

"Giles has only been engaged the once. His ex-fiancée married someone else a long time ago, so there's no need to worry about her."

"Have you no interest in marriage, Lord Russel?" Not wanting to hear anything more about Giles's previous engagement, she changed the subject to Richard.

"Me? Not quite yet. What about you, though? Have you never been engaged before this potential betrothal to the childhood friend of yours?"

"No. I do not possess a dowry," she told him with a smile, but he stared at her in surprise.

Huh? That's strange. Surely, he knows my family is poor. Dowries were essential for marriage between nobles. They were but a piece of the trousseau a bride took with her to her new home, to serve as her fortune and to support her in-laws. Of course, the larger the dowry was, the more advantageously she could marry. And if a dowry could not be prepared, then marriage was impossible.

The Clayburns had sold all their jewels to pay off their medical expenses. They had no extra funds with which to provide an adequate dowry for their daughters. On the other hand, when a man was adopted into the family of the bride, it was his family who paid a dowry. This was why House Hayes took on a portion of the construction fees for the river, and it had to be one of the reasons her father was so concerned with her taking a husband. *Though I would sooner ask Cecilia to be the one to take a husband.* Fiona could support herself by working. She had no reason to force herself to remain at home.

"Now I get it," Richard said.

While a woman with no dowry could temporarily take a lover, she could not become engaged or be wed. Fiona had assumed Richard was aware of this when he suggested that she and Giles pretend to be a couple—that Giles would have no need to worry she would urge him to marry her because, even if she did, it could never happen.

Nonetheless, Richard stared fixedly at her, another smile that held something back from her spread across his face. "Well, I'm sure you'll be able to make it all work out somehow."

Make what work out? she wanted to ask, but the song came to an end.

While Richard seemed to consider the whole affair a great source of amusement, Fiona could tell that he sincerely cared about Giles. The proof was in how readily Giles accepted his advice. The two of them had known each other and been friends since they were children. Being high-ranking nobles meant limitations on who you associated with even from infancy; they were lucky to have built such a close friendship.

As Fiona and Richard exchanged courtesies at the end of the song, Giles returned to them, which brought a crooked smile to Richard's face. "Say, Gil, didn't you come back a little too quickly?"

"So what if I did?"

These two sure are such nice friends.

Giles drew her by the hand again as the three of them left the dancing circle.

Caroline's heels clicked loudly as she walked down the empty halls of the back of the estate. Her followers and her lady's maids were instructed not to follow her—she was in no mood to hear their empty words and flattery.

"Who does that drab woman think she is?" She had waited so long for this party, and Giles was supposed to be dancing with her. She had planned to be with him not for a single dance or two, but to hang onto him for the entire night.

Even if she shut her eyes or shook her head in denial, she couldn't get the way Giles smiled at Fiona out of her head. That smile—and everyone's attention—should have been hers.

This can't be happening. There's something wrong with this situation!

That woman was not a beauty, nor did she come from a powerful family. Caroline knew that her own physical figure and dress were far superior. And yet—! She snapped her fan shut with displeasure she could no longer hold back.

"Pardon me, my lady, but I would like to speak with you."

Caroline didn't recognize the mellow voice. "Who are you?" She stopped and turned to find a tall man standing before her.

He had long brown hair tied at his collar. His handsome features and smart dress gave him the appearance of a noble, but there was something about him that came off as pretentious, especially for one of her guests. However, Caroline was too agitated to notice.

"I have a request concerning the woman at Lord Lowell's side. Would you be willing to speak with me about her for a moment?"

Caroline answered his suspicious, thin-lipped smile with a glare.

After she finished dancing with Richard, some people came over to talk to Fiona. However, they were all acquaintances from the gallery and people who wanted to speak with Giles about work. Not a single woman came over to air their jealous grievances or harass her.

I feel both relieved yet also kind of let down? But this is definitely a good thing! She had braced herself for the worst, and while she celebrated the peacefulness, there was another part of her that questioned the meaning of her presence here.

Giles took it upon himself to tell anyone who asked her to dance that her dance card was full, so she didn't even need to decline anyone herself. With Richard in the mix, they ate, drank, and looked at the paintings hanging at the venue.

When he saw them looking with great interest at portraits of the various generations of his family, the Earl of Burleigh himself made his way over to give them a thorough explanation. It seemed his daughter Caroline had no interest in her family's history or works of art beyond decorations. Fiona noticed Giles giving her a crooked smile at how well she and the earl hit it off.

The rest of the party passed harmoniously. Eventually, she found herself in the carriage on her way home. As soon as the carriage began to move, Giles took a close look at her face.

She must have looked unhappy, because he asked, "Are you tired?"

"A bit, but I had a great deal of fun. I'm glad that nothing happened while we were there," Fiona said candidly, making Giles chuckle again. He was still in good spirits.

"Were you hoping there would be trouble?"

"N-not exactly. I couldn't help but notice that Lady Caroline never came back, though."

"Now that you mention it, you're right." Lady Caroline had been their primary concern for the evening, but Giles made it sound like he had forgotten about her entirely.

"Did you actually forget about her?"

"Yeah, I suppose I did, once she left the hall."

Caroline probably wouldn't believe it from the way she relentlessly attacked him, but Giles clearly felt nothing for her. *It's not that there's anything that can be done about it, and while I do feel sorry for her...* Truly, as a woman of Caroline's age, she couldn't help but have some sympathy for her. However, if she were in Giles's position, she would want Caroline to cut it out as well.

Fiona gave a slight shake of her head in disbelief of Giles's disregard for Caroline, causing a tuft of her done-up hair to fall to her shoulder. Giles scooped it up automatically and tucked it behind her ear.

Her breath caught in her throat. This was the kind of behavior that he really needn't bother with when they didn't have an audience. It still took her by surprise, so he kept doing it even when no one was looking—a way for her to practice. She told herself that he was just treating her like a pet dog.

While she no longer showed it so much on her face, it was still hard to stop her heart from reacting to his touch. In terms of who was the better actor, Fiona really did lose to him. She wanted to behave more like they were a couple, but she struggled to determine just how to do that.

"Perhaps I should've gotten you matching earrings," Giles murmured to himself as his fingers retreated from her unadorned earlobe. The only accessories Fiona was wearing were the ring and a small choker that she borrowed from her grandmother.

"N-no, you don't have to go out of your way like that."

"Are you sure?"

"Yes! Besides, if you did, the ring won't stand out so much anymore." Fiona held up both of her hands to ward him off, desperate to convince him. She really didn't want any more lavish gifts.

Giles gave her a small nod of understanding. "I see."

To cover up her restlessness, Fiona changed the subject. "A-anyway, I expected something would happen to me. Perhaps being called over to an unoccupied corner where someone would spill wine on my dress or something like that."

She figured that since she was good at running, she would be safe—so long as she knew the route to the powder room—and could take care of any stain before it dried. At this stage, it was a groundless fear, but she had been prepared all the same.

Giles tried—and failed—to hold back his laughter at Fiona's carefully thought-out strategies. "I think you've been reading too many of those novels."

Fiona turned away in a huff. "It's not nice to laugh like that."

"I'm sorry. But I guess you must not trust me very much if you imagine something terrible will happen at places I take you."

"That's not what I was implying." She had braced herself because she had heard that Caroline was ruthless. Her head whipped back around to tell him it was not a matter of her trust in him, when her eyes met Giles's.

His expression relaxed. "That's not to say that things will always go so smoothly. It feels inappropriate to apologize or thank you for this, but you really did help me out tonight."

His eyes conveyed none of the merriment she kept seeing in them at the party. She could see as much even in the dimly lit carriage. All the while, her heart beat quietly away.

It wasn't as if people weren't speaking ill of her behind her back. Fiona simply chose to ignore that fact. She had been prepared for it as a consequence of being at Giles Bancroft's side; they would have spoken ill no matter who the woman was.

Of course, Giles had factored that into his plans for the evening. That was why Fiona was never alone the whole time they were at the party. Richard had been there to back them up as well. The looks people gave her softened, to some degree, after she finished dancing with him.

Giles was going out of his way to be very considerate, more than was necessary for their charade. She needed no apology or thanks, but hearing him thank her with such a serious look on his face left her at a loss for words.

"I'm going to ask you to accompany me to other parties from now on as well."

"Y-yes, of course."

"And next weekend is the party at your estate, correct?" He said it as if it were the most natural thing in the world, surprising her utterly.

"What?"

Giles frowned at her reaction. "Did you not want me to attend?"

Her engagement to Norman was postponed for the time being. Besides, news of their relationship had already spread to a remarkable extent; there was no need to further reinforce those rumors by having him attend the party at her estate. She doubted Giles wanted some baron from the far-off countryside to be part of his circle of acquaintants.

Until then, he hadn't said much on the subject. That was why she assumed that he would not be attending.

"It's not that I don't want you to attend, um..."

"I wouldn't be so irresponsible as to *not* attend."

"I'm sorry for assuming as much."

"I thought it was a given. That was why I never brought it up." Giles sat back in his seat, uncrossing and recrossing his legs. He stared quietly ahead in protest, as though he were sulking.

"But if you come, then that'll just cause more—"

"What? Lend more credibility to the rumors? That's what we want."

Her best friend Olga would be there. Fiona had no idea how she could face her with Giles on her arm. Although she had been fine walking around town with him, and even accompanying him to an earl's party, for some reason she felt nervous about attending an event at her home with him.

"At any rate, I will be there," Giles concluded. All Fiona could do was nod.

Wait, if Lord Giles comes to the party, then... Perhaps she could introduce them. Fiona's mood brightened as she struck upon the idea. "Um, Lord Giles?"

"Yes?" Even his tone was sulky. She felt bad for making him feel ostracized, but for some reason, she found his inability to hide his displeasure cute.

"I'm sorry. Please let me apologize. I do not mean to come off as untrusting or imply that I do not think I can count on you. It's just that I hadn't expected you to go so far to fulfill your role in our agreement."

"Then isn't that proof that you don't trust me?"

"This I cannot deny. And I'm sorry for that." If she were in his place, she too would feel inadequate.

Her honest recognition of her mistake and subsequent apology seemed to help lighten the mood a little. "We may be from different social positions," Giles said, "but you needn't exercise such thorough discretion with me."

"You're the only one who would say that."

"Fiona—"

"Very well. There is something I would ask of you, then. Would you please invite Uncle Talbott to our party?"

"You mean Lord Talbott?"

"Yes." Surprised, Giles leaned forward again and turned to face her. "It would not be proper for a mere baron to send an invitation to the former prime minister," Fiona explained. "But if he happened to drop by as your companion, then...it would not seem so unnatural."

"I see. I'm only just acquainted with him, though."

"I shall write to him first. All you need to do on the day is stop by his home. If he declines, then that's that."

As far as rank was concerned, Giles was a suitable companion for Lord Talbott. However, while he was once the prime minister, Lord Talbott only associated with a particular circle of nobles. Since stepping down the previous year, he lived as a private individual and rarely showed up at balls, out of consideration for the influence of his long-earned accomplishments.

However, Fiona had a feeling he would come to her family's party. "I'm sorry, but I cannot give you the full particulars. But there's nothing shameful about it, I promise you." Her serious, earnest voice rang out in the carriage, her amber eyes reflecting the flickering light.

"I cannot guarantee that he will accept, but I don't mind inviting him so long as you acknowledge that."

"Of course! Thank you so much!" Fiona broke out into a broad smile, which made Giles smile as well. To herself, Fiona whispered, "Won't you be so happy, Marianne?" The sound of her voice was drowned out by the sound of the turning wheels.

Fiona rocked and swayed. She didn't feel like she was standing or like she was sitting in a chair. Nothing supported her, but she felt a curious sense of security, wrapped up snugly as she was.

This rocking was not that of a carriage, which meant... *Am I on a boat?* Perhaps she was on a boat with her uncle, leaving the country. Her dream had come true.

Where were they going? What would they see? Before anything else, she wanted to see the vast ocean with her own two eyes. She felt so happy and had looked forward to this for so long...and yet, for some reason, her heart ached.

The sound of knocking woke her. "Sister? Are you awake?"

A familiar ceiling; a familiar bed. Morning light shone through the thin curtains. Fiona was in her own room.

As she pulled down the sheet to sit up, her eye caught sight of the glittering yellow diamond ring. She looked up and met the gaze of her sister, who was peeking in from behind the door. Cecilia sighed with relief as she entered.

"I just woke up now." Fiona sat up, holding her foggy head.

Cecilia approached at once to examine her. "I still cannot believe that you fell asleep in the carriage on your way home. We were all shocked when Lord Lowell stepped out of the carriage carrying you in his arms."

"He did what?!"

They had all assumed that she had fallen ill suddenly, but she was only fast asleep in his arms.

"He said that he didn't want to wake you since you were sleeping so soundly. He told us that you must have been exhausted since you're not used to parties. Then he carried you all the way to your bed."

"H-he did?"

"He certainly did."

Fiona had no memory of it. She remembered talking about the party at her house and asking Giles to invite Lord Talbott. She thought she remembered talking about something insignificant next, but after that, her memory was hazy.

Fiona did remember how nice the swaying of the carriage felt. *I think I had a dream about being on a boat?* She would've never imagined that she was actually being carried in Giles's arms—and in front of her whole family, no less!

Perhaps she should hide under the blankets. Fiona's face flushed bright red from embarrassment, making Cecilia laugh. Since Cecilia looked so much like their mother, it felt like her mother was laughing at her, making Fiona even more embarrassed.

"Breakfast is ready. You should come downstairs and assure Father and Hans that you're well."

"Nngh, I shall."

They went to their first party as a couple, managed to convince everyone, and thwarted Lady Caroline. Fiona must have lost consciousness because she was so relieved that they managed to clear such a high hurdle. However, whatever the circumstances may have been...

"How could I?!" As soon as her sister left the room, Fiona plunged her face into her pillow.

CHAPTER 9

Marianne and Lord Talbott

"**H**OW ARE YOU FEELING, Fiona?"

"I am well, Father."

"I-is that so?"

Fiona carried on smiling at her strangely worried father throughout breakfast, all the while feeling Hans's watchful gaze on her. When she finished eating, she returned to her room to write.

She prepared two papers and envelopes and wrote to Lord Talbott, the former prime minister, and her good friend Marianne. As she wrote, she fondly remembered Marianne's cute little baby. "It's been a whole year. Her baby must've grown so much by now."

She had only met Marianne the previous year, shortly after her family's annual arrival in the capital. Once the townhouse was ready, Fiona and Hans headed to Roche's gallery on Bay Street. They rode in a carriage and stopped near the gallery to walk the rest of the way, saying hello to the owners of the stores they passed.

That was when Fiona noticed a woman in an abnormal state. Her steps were unsteady, and she kept stopping to breathe heavily. "Hans, does that woman seem unwell to you?"

"Oh my, I think you're right. Oh!" As he spoke, the woman staggered over to the wall of a shop and crumpled to the ground.

They rushed over to her and found that the woman was about the same age as Fiona. Her breathing was labored. "Th-the baby…"

It wasn't obvious from behind, and with her slim stature, but the woman cradled a big, pregnant belly. Her face was as white as a sheet, and sweat dripped down it as they helped her stand back up. Fiona called desperately for help and for a doctor. They were next to the gallery, so Roche heard the commotion and came running.

She was not yet full-term, but after a long labor, the woman gave birth to an adorable baby girl. The woman's name was Marianne, and she said that her only relation was her husband. The proprietress of a nearby shop said she knew Marianne, and that her husband was a soldier who would not return for another month yet.

Marianne's life was in danger due to the child's premature birth, but she tried to leave the hospital after they were done treating her. The hospital urged her to stay until her husband's return, but she didn't have any more money to pay the hospital, and she was adamant that she would not go to the abbey.

However, the woman could barely stand, let alone carry her baby in her arms. The people of the town pitied her—but the social dictates there were unlike those of the countryside, where everyone had to help one another to get by. People knew only her name and address; no one was willing to take in, and care for, a woman and her newborn babe.

If this happened on our land, things would be different.

There were misfortunate people everywhere. One couldn't extend help to everyone. Moreover, this was the capital, and Marianne was not one of their citizens. In her head, Fiona understood the logic of quietly overlooking those in need since she didn't have the means to help everyone equally.

But now that she was involved, Fiona couldn't simply ignore this woman. She couldn't help but compare this woman to her own mother who had died just after childbirth. Besides, Marianne was only a year older than her. It must've been fate that brought them together.

"I have a room you can rest in, although it's not a hospital bed."

"I knew you would say as much, Miss Fiona," said Hans.

Fiona brought Marianne and her baby, somewhat forcefully, back to the Clayburns' townhouse. In an environment with ample food where she could recuperate in peace, Marianne made a slow recovery.

Up to that point, Marianne had worked as a maid, doing cleaning and cooking. However, when given activities as a means of whiling time away during her recovery, she showed that she was proficient with embroidery and could read aloud without any mistakes. She also had manners that differed from those of commoners, and sometimes she slipped into using an accent that was not typical of people who grew up downtown. All things considered, it was hard to believe that she grew up where they had found her.

Fiona assumed she had reason to hide her origins, but it didn't take long to find out her history. While Fiona and her family didn't pry, Marianne eventually opened up to them: she was the daughter of Prime Minister Talbott, and she had eloped with her boyfriend in an act of rebellion against her family. She told them this because her husband, Kyle, would return the following month.

Fiona suggested that she at least inform her father about his grandchild's birth, but Marianne refused. "He will never accept our relationship. I just know that he'll force us apart, even if we do have a child now." Marianne insisted reconciliation was impossible unless he was willing to meet them halfway. In the face of such resolve, Fiona felt she could not say anything more.

Later, Marianne's husband Kyle said, "I love Marianne. I do not regret marrying her, but I feel all I have given her is a life of hardship. If you were to ask me if I made the right decision, I could not rightly say yes." Kyle had been in the military for many years by that point. He owned a shop in the countryside that he had cashed out his pension to buy. Because Marianne refused to reach out to her family, and Kyle believed he needed to make a name for himself before mending that bridge, the two of them sadly went home with the babe in her mother's arms.

Not long thereafter, Lord Talbott came to Gallery Roche as a customer. It turned out that he had been secretly searching for his runaway daughter all this time. It was hard to track her down because she kept changing her address; when he discovered a small house that she and Kyle had rented, it was already vacated. He lost the trail after that and later braced for the worst when he caught wind that a woman who looked like his daughter had collapsed on Bay Street. He learned from the proprietress of a nearby store that Fiona had helped his daughter, which led him to the gallery.

It was a bit early for guests to begin arriving for the party. Fiona was already dressed and stationed in front of the gate, nervously awaiting Marianne's arrival at the Clayburns' house.

"Oh, Marianne!"

"It's been far too long."

They ran toward each other as soon as they spotted one another, and they exchanged the hugs that they couldn't share through letters.

"I'm glad to see you looking well!"

Marianne smiled shyly. "You too." Her complexion looked much healthier than it had been when she left the previous year.

"It's nice to see you all again."

"Oh, Kyle, no need to be so formal with us. Wow, Flora! You've grown so big!"

Baby Flora had soft golden hair. She looked like an angel in her father's arms, as she eagerly reached out her small hands toward Fiona.

"I tried to put a ribbon in her hair for the occasion, but she wound up pulling it out. I guess it bothered her."

"She's still adorable, if you ask me," Fiona declared.

"Hee hee. Yes, she is!" Marianne giggled as she followed Fiona into the house where Cecilia and the others waited.

"Sister, I want to see the baby!"

"Hold on, Cecilia. Grandpa Clayburn should be the one to hold her first."

"My lord—"

"What? It's fine if I hold a baby, Hans!"

Every member of the Clayburn family adored children. They swarmed around the new arrivals. Flora was not normally shy, but seeing such a large number of people crowd around her at once made her bury her face in Kyle's chest.

"Aww, so cute!" gushed Fiona and Cecilia. They found delight in everything the small girl did.

The party that night was a gathering of friends, so Fiona didn't feel the need to dress up lavishly to impress: she wore a slightly more casual dress than the one she wore to the Earl of Burleigh's ball. Not yet of age, Cecilia would only drop in briefly to say hello, so she wore the same kind of dress she always did.

Marianne was dressed up nicely, but she had a familial air to her, like she was going to a birthday party. Flora didn't seem nervous, but she let out a big yawn and was soon taken to an upstairs guest room that wouldn't be used for the party.

Fiona and Marianne stepped away as the others crowded around the sleeping baby.

"Thank you for today, Fiona."

"You're welcome. I'm sure he'll be here." Fiona leaned in close to Marianne, who still seemed a bit uneasy. "I hear from Mr. Roche that you still have that painting."

"I would never sell the first gift Flora ever received. Besides, that seamstress job you introduced me to has been a great source of income."

"That's all because of your skill. I'm sure that Mrs. Bennett must be strict."

"She's finally started giving me work besides accessories. Hee hee, as it so happens, the dress I'm wearing now is my test piece. They let me borrow it." Marianne pinched the hem of the dress, which had an embroidered neckline.

"Is that so? Your embroidery is a marvel."

Mrs. Bennett's shop employed a select few seamstresses. Knowing Marianne's skill, Fiona introduced her, and after a trial period, Marianne was now firmly counted among their numbers.

It was a job she could do at home while looking after her baby. While she was only paid for each piece she finished, the compensation was good. Kyle had also received a small promotion in the military, and now Marianne was able to smile cheerfully, confident that their circumstances were more stable.

"Say, did you know that my embroidery will be on a certain someone's dress that's being sewn right now?" Marianne whispered proudly, attempting to keep herself together as she waited anxiously for her reunion with Lord Talbott.

"Oh?"

"That Lord Lowell really does have his eye on you."

"W-wait, how—?"

"There's no need to get all bashful about it."

Oh, that's right. Of course she would know! Maison de Michele was Marianne's place of employment. She would've heard about the visit Fiona and Giles paid the shop, whether the employees were intentionally gossiping or not. Fiona fanned her burning cheeks with her hand, feeling self-conscious.

But now that I think about it, Marianne might be knowledgeable on how to effectively be someone's sweetheart. Fiona had yet to find anyone else to turn to, so she remained at a loss for how to match Giles. Surely Marianne, who had been so passionately in love that she eloped, would have some advice.

Fiona decided to ask. "Say, could I ask you to give me some advice?"

"Hee hee hee! Yes, you can ask me anything. What is it you'd like to know? Good places for dates where no one will see you? Ciphers to use when writing letters? How to sneak home without getting caught? I'll tell you how to do anything you want!" Marianne confidently patted her chest and Fiona knew she would be in good—

No, wait. That wasn't the sort of thing she wanted to know at all. "I think I am beginning to sympathize with Lord Talbott."

"Oh, really?"

The pair of them carried on giggling and blushing until the party began.

Lord Talbott himself opened the front door when Giles arrived, eager with anticipation. He was already prepared to go, so they proceeded directly to the carriage and set off for the Clayburns' house as if it were just another day.

Giles informed him of their destination, just in case; he knew only that he was to ask Lord Talbott to join him but not exactly why. Lord Talbott nodded in response. Giles had no intention of demanding an explanation, but during the trip, Lord Talbott filled him in. After hearing Lord Talbott's tale, he understood why Fiona had been hesitant to divulge any details.

He had heard that Lord Talbott's daughter was at home on their land recovering from illness. It would've been imprudent of Fiona if she had told Giles that the young woman had, in fact, eloped with a common soldier. She had done well to keep it secret.

"At the time, she refused to let me take the initiative in speaking with my daughter."

"Fiona did?"

"That's right. When I visited the gallery during my investigation, she told me I would have to come myself if I wanted to see my daughter and granddaughter. Goodness, what a strong-willed woman she is."

Having seen how Fiona confronted Gordon in Giles's parlor, without asking for anyone's aid, Giles could picture her speaking candidly even to the prime minister—though picturing it made his brow break out in a cold sweat.

"It's a complicated matter, not the sort of thing that can resolved by a person or two acting as intermediary. However, she is about the same age as Marianne. She told me how Marianne felt about the matter, and what's more, she went on and on about how adorable my granddaughter is. That made me feel even worse." Lord Talbott chuckled in self-deprecation, looking far older than Giles remembered him looking at the assembly hall. His expression, however, was much softer than it used to be. "She told me of how deep my daughter and her husband's love is for one another, which was disconcerting, as you can imagine. A soldier may die at any time. And I had Marianne very late in my life. If I were to die and she lost her husband as well, who would be there to protect her?"

"Hmm."

"But I suppose the fact of the matter is that she didn't need anyone's protection to begin with." What Marianne wanted was not a protector to lead her by the hand but a partner to walk with through the hardships of life. Lord Talbott reluctantly admitted that it was Fiona who made him realize that. "When I said that I could not pardon what they'd done but I did want to help, she flatly dismissed me, saying that they wouldn't take my money. I can't say she was wrong, though."

"What an incorruptible heart she has."

"Hmph, it's just stubbornness. I could tell that she and Marianne are of the same mold. Fiona recommended that I buy a painting instead of giving Marianne money."

"A painting?" It wasn't an unusual suggestion, given that they were speaking at an art gallery, but pushing a sale during such a conversation didn't seem like the sort of thing Fiona would do.

But Lord Talbott gave a crooked smile as he said admiringly, "She suggested I give the painting to Marianne as a present for the birth of the child. Fiona promised me that they would refund the money I spent to Marianne if she came in to sell it. Ha ha, the surprised look on the gallery owner's face when she suggested that!"

"Ah, I understand now." Fiona must have assumed that, while Marianne might refuse money, she would not reject a gift for her daughter. That gift could be converted into money if necessary. While the end result was the same, the impression upon receiving such a gift would be very different.

Giles was impressed that a young noblewoman like Fiona came up with such an idea. Then he remembered her mentioning that she had experienced financial hardships.

It had nothing to do with age or gender. Though she was five years younger than him, she had experienced many things that Giles hadn't. The thought made him strangely anxious.

"She picked out a portrait of the Virgin Mary and baby Jesus. Mary looked a bit like my late wife. I am ashamed to admit it, but it felt like that was the first time I ever properly saw a painting."

"I see."

"Originally, I planned to visit Marianne again after I resigned... However, I have yet to do so. And now I have received this invitation. She has helped me out yet again," Lord Talbott muttered to himself as he gazed out the window. After a short silence, Lord Talbott thumped the floor of the carriage with his cane as if an idea just occurred to him. "She refused to let me pay for the expenses of taking care of my daughter and her baby—she said it was only letting a friend sleep over at her house. So that's why I insisted on writing a letter of introduction for her. And I hear she used that to meet with you, Lord Lowell."

"That is correct. She used it to return something I lost, since we did not then know one another."

"Hmph. I can hardly say I'm surprised she would use it for that. But I suppose this means that it's all thanks to me that you two were brought together."

"I suppose you could say that." Without the letter of introduction, Giles would've refused to meet her, even after she traveled all that way to his home. They were where they were now thanks to her managing to cross such a tightrope. It sounded implausible, but it was true.

"What a boring answer." Lord Talbott thumped his cane again, rapidly changing the mood in the carriage. A chill ran down Giles's spine as he felt the immensity of Lord Talbott's stature, his long years serving at the heart of complicated politics. With a sharp glint in his eye, Lord Talbott said, "You should part with her immediately if you cannot treasure her as she deserves. I can find her plenty of suitable potential husbands to choose from."

He spoke as if Giles were the man who ran off with his daughter. The man's presence was overwhelming, and Giles's instincts told him that he must not falter. "I am afraid I must ignore your warning."

"I'll be watching you."

After an exceptionally tense ride, they arrived at the Clayburns' townhouse.

CHAPTER 10

The Party at the Clayburn Residence

THE PARTY AT THE Clayburn residence was accented by the chef's best cooking and flowers, painstakingly grown by the baron himself.

All the invitees were acquaintances of the family. The mood was that of a fun get-together, rather than a gathering for nobles, so everyone got on amiably.

"I missed you so much, Fiona!"

"Thank you so much for coming, Olga!"

They joined hands, as thrilled to see one another as if it had been a year since their last meeting; in truth, it was half a month ago at the prince's party. So many things had happened in the span of a single week that Fiona felt like a full month had passed. It felt even longer to her friend Olga, who had been hearing rumors about Fiona's sensational love life but hadn't had a chance to see her. They wrote to one another, but it wasn't the same: Olga felt she had been waiting for an eternity to finally talk to Fiona about it all.

Olga was the daughter of Viscount Symonds, and Fiona had been acquainted with her and her family for about ten years.

She was a valuable source of information about the goings-on of high society, and she was also the woman who had given Fiona the romance novels. It was because of her love for dramatic stories that Olga loved gossip, but she was not the type to impose her own judgment, believing that it was not her place. She mainly liked to collect information because she enjoyed comparing different pieces of rumors and trying to puzzle out the true story. Overall, she liked thinking about people's relationships. And Fiona liked how readily Olga admitted as much.

"Come, Fiona. Let us speak over there."

"All right," Fiona agreed, and Olga happily led her over to a couch in a corner of the room.

Fiona had asked Giles to arrive at the party a little later than everyone else. His arrival meant that she would have to stick by his side, so now was her only real chance to talk with Olga.

"Your dress is so cute. It reminds me of poppies," Fiona said earnestly as she sat down.

Olga was wearing an orange dress that flared at the bottom. It brought out the color of her dark hair. Olga winked one of her light brown eyes from behind her spectacles. "Hee hee, thank you. And you look lovely as well."

"You think so? I'm dressed the same as always."

They were close enough that such compliments weren't necessary for the sake of politeness, so perhaps Olga really did think so—but Fiona wasn't sure why. She had yet to receive her new dress from Michele, so she had simply paired different accessories with one of her old dresses. Different accessories were hardly enough to make a drastic impact in how this dress appeared, and she was dressed less extravagantly than she had been for the celebration at the royal palace. Yet Olga seemed more taken with this dress than the one she wore then.

"It's true what they say about love changing you. Speaking of which, how long have you and Lord Lowell been together?"

Fiona was prepared for the topic but still couldn't help laughing. "You're really just going to dive in like that?" Her friend was always straight to the point, but she leapt at this particular topic far more quickly than Fiona expected.

"Of course I am. I've heard so many rumors about your relationship, and yet I didn't know a single thing firsthand, even though we're friends! You have no idea how hard it's been for me to wait to speak with you."

"Just how many rumors are we talking about here?"

"It's the hottest topic in years! People are saying that fate brought you together."

"Th-they are?"

"Of course!" Olga said cheerfully. "This is Lord Lowell we're talking about, after all!" She placed her hands on her hips and whipped her brunette hair back.

Fiona knew there were rumors, but she hadn't expected them to go so far. She must've looked on the verge of shrinking back, because Olga kept a firm grip on her hand, preventing her retreat.

Olga's eyes gleamed as she leaned in closer. "Now, tell me! Where did you first meet?"

"We first met at the celebration for the prince. I ran into him in one of the smaller gardens just before I left."

"And then a mere two days later you went on a date in the park. And the weekend after that, you accompanied him to the Earl of Burleigh's ball, didn't you? It really does sound like destiny!"

"Stop making fun of me already."

Olga reverently lifted Fiona's hand to marvel at the yellow diamond ring. "It's so beautiful."

"Yes, though it's far too expensive for someone like me."

"Nonsense. It looks splendid on you. Lord Lowell certainly has a discerning eye."

"Yes, he does. For the extravagant."

"I don't mean the ring, Fiona. I mean you." The serious look Olga gave her took Fiona by surprise. Then, her expression changed to a wry smile. "For the entire time I've known you, you could be a bit slow at times. Or perhaps it's better to say that you're just not aware of it."

"What? Not aware of what?" Fiona genuinely didn't understand what her friend meant, but Olga only shrugged.

"Don't worry about that. Anyway, what else is there? Tell me everything!"

"Um, well..." Urged on by Olga's badgering, Fiona began to tell her the same story she had told her family.

Just as Olga's questions began to truly dig in deep, making Fiona break out in a cold sweat, there was a commotion from the entry hall. They turned to see that standing opposite of all their acquaintances was Giles—together with Lord Talbott.

Oh, thank goodness he came! Fiona had been certain that he would, but she was relieved to see it with her own eyes.

She stood up reflexively. Giles saw her and waved, and everyone turned in tandem to look at her.

"Olga, I..." Although they weren't done talking, Fiona had to go to him. Few guests at this party would be eager to make the acquaintance of an earl's son and the former prime minister; in fact, many seemed rather nervous about their presence. It wouldn't be fun for anyone if the new arrivals were stopped in the hall and everyone was forced to politely deal with one another, so Fiona decided to take them to another room.

It was an impolite thing to do with such high-ranking nobles, but for the two of them, the party was just a pretext. Lord Talbott was only there to see his daughter and her family, and Giles was only there for the sake of appearances.

Still cheerful, Olga waved Fiona off. "Don't worry about me! It's only natural that you would rather be with your beloved than your friend." Not that that was true. And while Olga urged her to go, she didn't let go of Fiona's hand. Instead, she began to recite in a lofty tone, "'His every move brings back the memory unbidden, the day he held me in his strong arms. The softness of his lips; the way he whispered sweet nothings in my—'"

"H-hey, Olga. What are you going on about?" Fiona was startled to find that she could relate to what Olga was saying.

"That was from Shirley Sandona's newest work, *Love in an Eternal Desert*. I'll be sure to lend it to you next time we meet!"

She was talking about a novel. Fiona was relieved but embarrassed at her own reaction. "Is that one about a princess too?"

"This one is about a dancer and a prince from a foreign country. But she's actually the illegitimate child of royalty. It's full of romance and drama!"

"She's basically a princess, then."

"So what?" Olga quipped. "Anyway, I'll speak more with you later. I'll always be on your side, you know. Remember that." She kissed Fiona on the cheek before she could respond, then gave her a light push. "Now, go to him!"

Fiona looked back several times as she walked away.

As Giles greeted his girlfriend, Olga was struck by how different he was from when he was still being called the Icy Scion. The way he smartly took Fiona's hand and drew her close to himself in one fluid motion, made them look like the picture-perfect couple.

Her back was turned, but Olga imagined that Fiona's cheeks were still flushed and that she wore a dazed smile.

"I've never seen Fiona acting this adorably before... However..." Fiona was hiding something, that much Olga could tell for certain. Fiona was candid by nature, but she was circumspect when it came to matters concerning other people. Perhaps that was why she couldn't speak openly yet. It was easy for Olga to imagine that not all was well in their relationship.

Giles, heir to the Earl of Bancroft, was from a distinguished family with a long history. Objectively speaking, Fiona's family status and reputation in society hardly made for a suitable match to him. It was likely that his relatives, and those around them, tolerated the relationship only because dating and marriage were entirely different matters in their eyes. They were overjoyed that Giles had finally taken an interest in dating after staunchly refusing the company of women for so long. They wouldn't approve so easily of anything beyond that, however.

Besides, Olga knew that Fiona was looking forward to going abroad with her uncle next year—she had been for years now. Marriage was never part of her plan. Whether their relationship only lasted the season or Fiona fell seriously enough for him to give up on her dream, as long as her friend was happy, Olga would be satisfied. On the other hand...

"You will pay dearly if you make her cry," Olga vowed quietly in the corner of the busy room.

"Thank you so much for coming tonight, Lord Talbott. It is most gracious of you."

"I apologize for turning up without a proper invitation."

"It is an honor and a privilege to have you here tonight. This is a modest gathering, but I hope you can relax and enjoy yourself." Fiona smiled from the heart, seeing how nervous

Lord Talbott appeared. His eyes searched the room, betraying his impatience.

Fiona exchanged a look with her father. They decided to escort him directly to the second floor where Marianne and her family waited.

"W-we have prepared a room for the two of you to rest in," Baron Clayburn said. "Come, Fiona."

"Yes, Father. This way, please." They led Lord Talbott and Giles up the stairs, just as they had planned. The volume of the party on the first floor dampened with each step.

As they walked down the narrow hallway, Lord Talbott said to Fiona, "It's nice to see you again."

"Yes, it's been a long time, hasn't it? I'm glad to see that you're the picture of health."

"Ha! I may have retired, but it'll be some time before I'm ready to kick the bucket."

"You'll have other kinds of happiness to look forward to from now on. I have a feeling you'll be even more busy than you were with your work." She smiled at Lord Talbott's scowl, then came to a stop in front of a guest room. She turned around and looked up at him; his expression was rigid. "Are you all right with this?"

"What problem could I have?"

"My apologies. Well then, I'll take Lord Lowell to the adjoining—"

"No, he can come with me." Fiona had expected it to be a private reunion between father and daughter. She glanced at Giles, who looked as surprised as she was. Lord Talbott muttered,

"I have explained the circumstances to him. There is no need to hide it."

His tone was miffed, but it was clear that he felt awkward about meeting his daughter and her family alone. Fiona said, "Would it be all right if I joined you as well, in that case?"

"Of course. You are my daughter's friend, after all."

Fiona exchanged a private look with Giles, and gave Talbott a small smile before knocking lightly on the door. As she opened it, a tense-looking Marianne and Kyle stood up to receive them. She stepped into the room, but Lord Talbott remained rooted to the spot.

"Father."

A long silence stretched out as father and daughter stood off against one another. Sweat began to form on Baron Clayburn's brow; he struggled with tense situations.

It was Marianne who broke the silence. She let out a breath and curtsied. Next to her, Kyle bowed deeply.

"It's been so long since we last saw each other. I see that you are still in good health, Father."

After a moment, Lord Talbott responded, "Yes."

Another silence fell then, but Lord Talbott stopped staring at his daughter and started looking around the room instead. This was probably as much of a compromise as Lord Talbott was willing to offer, so Fiona decided to help him out.

"Uncle Talbott, Flora is currently asleep."

"Oh. She is? After I came all this way... No, I won't say a thing."

Fiona couldn't resist the urge to tease that welled up inside her.

"When she's awake, Flora lives up to her name, the little flower fairy, but when she's asleep, she looks like an angel. Wouldn't you agree, Father?"

"Oh, uh, yes, I s-s-suppose?" Her father seemed startled to be addressed and stuttered as he agreed, earning himself a glare from Lord Talbott.

"She was starting to nod off while you were holding her earlier, wasn't she?"

"Y-yes, she was so cute."

"She snuggled right up to him, like this." Fiona cradled her arms and made a rocking motion, making her father smile.

"She snored so soundly too. Yes. Ah, she was adorable."

Lord Talbott began to grit his teeth as he watched their exchange. Giles kept his silence, but Fiona thought she caught sight of him pressing his fingers against his forehead.

And then there was a sudden, sweet cry. Fiona ignored how shaken Lord Talbott was and hurried over to the sofa. "Oh, is she awake?"

She peered into the small cradle and said in a melodic voice, "Good morning, Flora. Aww, you're cute when you're just waking up too. Here comes your mommy."

Flora started making cute grunts as she stretched her arms up. Marianne carefully scooped Flora up in her arms. "Come, Flora. Grandfather is here to see you."

"Daaah?" The golden-haired baby sucked on her thumb as she turned her face to Lord Talbott, who stood frozen as he gazed with intensity at Flora. "Ahh. Awwh."

She must've had a nice dream to have woken up in such a great mood. Flora looked about the room, waving her free hand.

"You're meeting so many new people today. Will you let one of them hold you?"

"I'd love to." Without missing a beat, Baron Clayburn began to move closer.

"You what?!" Lord Talbott rushed forward as well. "Wh-why are you—?"

"Do you need to ask? Children are treasures."

"Flora, would you rather the nice man hold you before grandpa gets his chance?"

"What?!"

At Marianne's words, both Flora's true grandfather and the would-be grandpa turned to glare at Giles. Giles realized he must be the "nice man" and flinched. "No, that's all right. Please."

"Hmph."

Fiona and Marianne burst out laughing, and even Kyle had to stifle a laugh. Although he blocked the baron and managed to approach, Lord Talbott stopped about a step away from his daughter. Thinking he might need one last push, Fiona was about to say something when he murmured, "She looks just like Lilianna."

It seemed Flora looked like his late wife, making him keenly aware of their blood relation. Marianne jumped, startled, and then began to gently rock Flora. "Isn't she cute?"

"Yes. She has a noble face."

"Mother was most ladylike."

"Indeed. Which makes me wonder who you took after," Lord Talbott said with a sigh. He was speaking from the heart, but his tone was not critical or scolding.

Lord Talbott sat gently on the sofa, and Marianne placed the round baby on his lap. Flora looked at him with her adorable, large, marine-colored eyes—the same color as his own. The unfamiliar shape of her ears was likely from her father's side.

"Da-ooh." Flora inclined her head and stretched out her tiny hand.

He couldn't tell if she wanted him to pick her up or to touch his beard, but an indescribable feeling welled up in Lord Talbott's chest. Marianne knelt beside them, smiling at the delicate way he held her daughter. She declared, "Who do I take after? Why, you, of course, Father."

"Yes, I suppose that's right. How troublesome."

"It's not troublesome. It's the reason that I'm so happy right now."

Lord Talbott slowly raised his arms to embrace both Marianne and Flora. Light glinted off the corners of his eyes. Kyle looked at Fiona, who took her father by the hand and pulled him away.

When they reached the door, Giles had an indescribable look on his face. He and his older sister Miranda were familiar with one another, to an extent. But Giles spoke of his parents and other relatives with such disinterest that Fiona had the impression that he avoided them. She was certain that he didn't have a close relationship with his parents.

This was not uncommon among nobles, but Fiona's heart broke to see the yearning with which Giles gazed upon Marianne and her family. *I pity him.* Even though he possessed everything a person could desire—rank, good looks, education—it might've been preferable to be a child who could wail about what he wanted or didn't want.

What was it he felt as he looked at the scene before him? It would be arrogance to think that she knew, so she quietly took his hand. He entwined their fingers without meeting her gaze.

A moment later, Lord Talbott addressed Kyle in a low voice: "Your name was Kyle, wasn't it?"

Kyle, who had been watching on in silence, stood straight at attention. "Y-yes, sir! I-I owe you a great—"

Lord Talbott cut him off with a quick glare. "Never mind that for the moment." Marianne stiffened, afraid that her father might demand they divorce, but instead he said, "You must swear to me that you shall never leave your wife and child behind in this world."

His tone was even more grave than it was when he demanded explanations at assemblies. Everyone in the room gasped.

Having had his resolution brought into question, Kyle cast off his nerves and matched Lord Talbott's gravity. "That has always been my intention."

"Young people these days are so boring in their answers," Lord Talbott muttered. He glanced with distaste between Kyle and Giles.

Flora reached her tiny hands for his scowl. "Daah. Da-ooh." She pulled with all her strength on his beard, making Lord Talbott yelp. "Mm! Mmph!"

"Oh my." Marianne chuckled as baby Flora squealed with delight. "Beards are so new and interesting, aren't they?"

"Hee hee!" Fiona couldn't help but giggle at the sight. She looked up to find Giles smiling beside her as well. As they gazed into one another's eyes, Fiona's father stood next to them, fretfully stroking his own mustache.

"Ow, ow! Oof!"

"Now, now, Flora, let him go!"

Lord Talbott's eyes were full of tears from the pain, but his granddaughter wouldn't let go. Kyle stepped in to try to help, and the struggle to pry her fingers loose continued for some time.

CHAPTER 11

The Repercussions of Rumors

IT WAS THE NIGHT AFTER Fiona and Giles attended their first party together, the ball at the Earl of Burleigh's estate. After the gallery on Bay Street closed for the day, they received a visitor in their back conference room.

It was just the two of them in the room. Across from Roche, the owner of the gallery, sat the Earl of Bancroft's son, Giles, whose father was a renowned collector of paintings.

"It is an honor to have you stop by our establishment, Lord Lowell. Thank you so much for the flowers you sent the other day. They really brightened up the gallery, and we received many compliments from our clients."

"Don't mention it. I apologize for calling on you after hours."

"Not at all. If anything, it is I who must apologize for receiving you here."

Since Giles had been unable to see Fiona two days prior, he had decided to follow Richard's advice and send flowers. He sent flowers to the gallery instead of directly to Fiona, in order to privately contact Roche.

"If we could get right to it—"

"Yes. As I briefly explained in my response, it is just as Miss Fiona told you. Raymond Bailey's relatives are in possession of his painting of the common redpoll. I can confirm as much because I have seen it with my own two eyes."

Roche was a famous dealer in art circles. Although his gallery did not have a long history, he was lauded for his young and energetic spirit. Giles had heard that both artists and customers had good experiences with him, and it turned out that he even kept an index of Raymond's works for reference.

"As you can see from the index, his most recent finished work was last year. It has already been sold. He hasn't put out anything new yet this year, and there are many people waiting."

Roche had been relieved when he received word from Raymond that his newest work was nearly finished; he hoped to unveil it before the season was out. Raymond kept his identity a secret and avoided social contact. As Roche explained, Raymond had never made an appearance at gatherings in the artists' world, and he was unmotivated by money. It was difficult to imagine that he would entrust his works to another dealer.

"Moreover, I have never once heard Raymond, or anyone in his family, mention someone by the name of Gordon. His claims to have some kind of connection to Raymond are highly suspect."

"So it really is a fake, then."

"It is highly likely. Regardless of what others may say, I can vouch for Miss Fiona's appraising eye. She is even more knowledgeable of contemporary painters than I am."

"She's that much of an expert?" Giles knew that Fiona had extensive knowledge about paintings, but it was still surprising to hear of her expertise from Roche, whose principal occupation was art.

Miranda hadn't heard from Gordon since she demanded an appraisal from the royal academy. There was a waiting list for appraisals, but it was doubtful that the painting had been entrusted to the academy in the first place. When Giles asked his sister, she told him she had not met Gordon through a referral. No matter how he looked at it, it was unnatural how the man tried to sell paintings to families belonging to the same political faction without any standing connection.

However, Gordon's prices for his fake paintings were low for a swindler, and the majority of the checks he received had yet to be cashed. If it was not money he was after, then why was Gordon trying to palm off these fake paintings?

Giles had his suspicions, but no harm had come to him or his family, and it was the busiest season for both parliament and social engagements. He considered leaving it alone, but he had someone investigate Gordon's background out of an abundance of caution: it turned out that there was hardly any information to be found about the man, which just made him seem even more suspicious.

After discussing things with Richard, Giles decided to first find out whether the other paintings Gordon was selling were real. That was his purpose in meeting Roche.

"With all that in mind, and as per your request, Lord Lowell, I shall send Miss Fiona to appraise the paintings Otto Gordon has sold. I shall adjust her work accordingly and leave the scheduling of the visits to you."

"Thank you."

"I'll speak with her about this tomorrow, but I doubt she will refuse."

All the paintings had been purchased by nobles of viscount or higher ranking. Fiona couldn't just show up and ask to appraise their authenticity; the reputation and pride of the families were at stake. However, a visit from Giles—accompanied by her as his partner—would allow her to appraise the paintings without arousing suspicion. If nothing was wrong, then all would be well; they could broach the topic officially if she found anything suspicious.

After going over what they would do in the event of a fake, Roche put a letter with a broken seal on the table. "I would like you to take a look at this. I just received it today."

"What's this?"

There was nothing written on the envelope, not even the name of the sender. Giles frowned as he checked the contents of the letter. It contained slander about Fiona written in blotted ink.

"The party at the Burleighs' was last night, correct? It's easy enough to discover that she works here, but this is quick work indeed."

"Have they visited her home?"

"Hans is keeping an eye out, but he has reported nothing yet. I imagine it's only a matter of time, though."

Giles nodded slowly at Roche, who looked worried.

"This evening, one of our employees noticed a young woman lying in wait. I pray this does not escalate."

Fiona had not come to the gallery that day. Giles was relieved to hear that she hadn't bumped into the woman. He had anticipated conflict, but that did not mean he wasn't distressed by the situation. Fiona was the one being disparaged in the letter, but Giles was also involved. If anything, he should've taken the brunt of the damage.

From the contents of the letter, it sounded like a noblewoman had written it because she was unhappy about Giles's beloved. But was that really all it was? There was still a chance that someone had ulterior motives in writing this under the pretext of jealousy—and the way Gordon had glared at Fiona as he left the Bancroft estate was unsettling.

It was also odd that the gallery she worked at was targeted before her home. Roche seemed to have the same concerns. "There have been reports of unsavory characters frequenting Gordon's establishment. When Miss Fiona told me about the fake painting, I had encouraged her to bring an escort, but she refused."

"I'll continue looking for the person responsible and have someone posted outside until then."

"Thank you. And I shall entrust deliveries and the like to someone other than Fiona in the interim."

"Please do. And don't—"

"Don't worry. This is between you and me." Giles nodded with a stern expression and began ruminating over what they had discussed. Roche watched him for a moment and then said, in a lighter tone, "Oh yes, I nearly forgot. I will accept the recompense for the appraisal at the sum you suggested. However, there is one matter I would like to discuss."

"Is it not a sufficient sum?" Giles asked.

"It's more than sufficient! But I would like to ask that you pay the travel expenses to Miss Fiona directly. And do not feel the need to pay her in cash or check; you may pay her with food or by taking her to the theater." This unexpected request baffled Giles, but Roche grinned knowingly. "The opera house at the heart of the city is not to be missed. The interior design is magnificent, and she rarely gets the opportunity to go. I am sure that she will be pleased."

Giles could sense his affection for Fiona.

"But I am blessed," Roche continued. "All the people I've come to know are so kind." He remembered Fiona saying the same thing with that carefree smile on her face. Fiona had truly built bonds that had nothing to do with what she possessed or what benefits people could give to her.

None of the people with whom Fiona surrounded herself would want her to be put in danger by her relationship with Giles. Giles felt the same. Even if the agreement between them was limited in tenure, it didn't matter; he didn't want to be the reason she got hurt. "The opera house, you say?"

"You can pay me back for this by dropping by during business hours next time. Not only will it keep the other women away from Fiona, it would be great publicity for a beginner gallery like mine to be known as the place frequented by the son of the

Earl of Bancroft." The way he presented this offer did not come off as shrewd or brazen in the least. If anything, Giles found him trustworthy.

"Very well. I shall remember this."

"Excellent. All my employees will give you a warm welcome."

They stood up and gave one another knowing smiles as they shook hands. Giles left the gallery feeling that this was the beginning of a long acquaintance.

TRUE LOVE Fades Away When the Contract Ends

One Star in the Night Sky

The Ring and the Secret Garden

A FEW DAYS AFTER Fiona and Giles agreed to feign being in love, Fiona heard that Giles had arrived to pick her up. She rushed out of her room and down the stairs to meet him. Giles gave her a quizzical look before she was even close enough for them to stretch out their hands and touch.

"Where's your ring?" Giles bent to whisper in her ear as soon as she set foot on the first floor.

She reflexively grasped at her left hand. "Huh?" *I can't believe he noticed so quickly!*

The day before, on their way home from the tearoom, he took her to a boutique and gave her a ring. There was a great deal of back-and-forth about it, but in the end, it was entrusted into her care...and now she wasn't wearing it on her hand.

She had put it on and taken it off countless times earlier in the day and ultimately left it in a drawer. Giles had no apparent interest in women's fashion and had never made any remark about it. To think that this would be the first thing out of his mouth!

"I, uh, left it in my room."

"But why?"

Fiona averted her eyes from his scrutinizing gaze, trying to scrounge up an explanation. "Um, I'm just not used to wearing that sort of thing. I'm afraid I might bang it on something."

Not only was the ring beautiful, it was a perfect fit. Fiona was unaccustomed to wearing jewelry on her hand, however, so it made her uncomfortable. Furthermore, it was a rather large gem—sure to be scuffed if she wasn't careful. She hadn't been able to suppress the panic that rose in her during the short time it took her to get home, where she could finally take it off.

"So I was thinking I should only wear it during the party."

"Fiona."

"Y-yes?"

For some reason, he only had to say her name and guilt began to swell inside her. Fiona looked miserable as Giles explained, "If you ask me, you should be wearing it now, so that you can get used to it."

That's a fair argument! I know, I know! But still! "What if I somehow manage to scratch it?"

"If this gem is brittle enough to be scratched just because you bumped into something, then I would have to take that jeweler to court."

"You would?!" She looked up at him, shocked. He smiled at her.

As the days went on and their meetings continued, he had started smiling at her. He was almost like a completely different person from the Icy Scion she had first met at the prince's party.

Although she knew he only behaved this way toward her because she was playing the role of his girlfriend, she didn't know how to handle it.

Fiona's loss for words brought a quizzical look to Giles's face. "I told you not to worry so much about it getting scratched. Or perhaps I should give you my family's ring?"

"That's all right, I shall put it back on at once!" She fled back up the stairs to retrieve it from her room. Behind her, she heard muffled laughter.

I lost again. It's not a matter of logic, though, but emotion! Giles would undoubtedly be leading her by the nose again today. It was remarkable how brilliantly he had come to embody his role in such a short amount of time.

She was sure that Richard's advice played a big part in it, but Giles was likely a quick learner. Having witnessed it for herself, she knew he had earned his reputation for being multi-talented.

This was their fourth day spent together, including the one in the park. It was also their fourth excursion together. In other words, Fiona had been seeing him daily. Although they were going on dates to stir up rumors about themselves, she had never imagined that they would go out together so frequently.

Fiona was sure he was a very busy man, and she doubted his claims that their spending so much time together was unproblematic for him. *We promised that we wouldn't force one another to do anything unreasonable. Even if he's simply following Lord Russel's advice, then that proves that Giles has a rather serious, or perhaps I should say faithful, character.*

But she thought it was probably because of his personality that he struggled to deal with all the potential matches offered to him. That meant that these outings, as opportunities to show as many people as possible that they were dating, were more important for him than for her. After all, rumors were his greatest defense in fending off potential suitors.

Meanwhile, Giles coming to meet Fiona at her home was plenty effective for her purposes. It had a strong impact on Fiona's father, and Fiona had heard from Norman that they were already planning to delay the engagement announcement. She had confirmed that they were only planning to hold one soirée at their house this season, which meant that while her engagement to Norman wasn't completely canceled, she had succeeded in buying herself the time she needed.

Now I just have to weather the season. Of course, I'm happy to go along with helping Lord Giles out, but I mustn't forget my place. She was playing a part.

Whenever he threw her for a loop by acting like her beau, she found herself paralyzed and unable to properly play along. Fiona tried her best, but she consistently felt defeated in the face of Giles, who seemed to pull it off effortlessly. And then there was the fact that he seemed to find her inability to react amusing.

For now, I just need to focus on playing my role well at the Earl of Burleigh's party. Fiona was confident that, if they could overcome this nearest and tallest peak, things would be smooth sailing afterward. She was trying to convince herself of this as she opened the dresser drawer and put the ring back on her finger.

Caroline had strong inclinations toward Giles, and Fiona was sure Caroline would see her as some annoying country bumpkin. Given Fiona's lower status, she might be seen as just a regular companion when she showed up to the party with Giles—and there was always the possibility that Caroline wouldn't acknowledge her existence in the first place.

Fiona could not afford to be brushed aside like she had been in the castle's garden. That was why it was crucial that she and Giles sow as many rumors about themselves as possible before the party—and then appear to be wrapped up in one another at the ball itself.

Neither of us have any dating or acting experience, and yet he outshines me in both, Fiona thought, frustrated, as she returned to the entrance hall.

Giles came to stand on her left. Previously, he was always at her right, to help support her injured foot.

"Your foot seems better today."

"Yes, it's much better." Fiona blinked as he took her left hand. "Um, what are you doing?"

He fit her hand snugly around his arm and brushed his fingers against the ring, smiling with satisfaction. "Since you're so worried about bumping it into something, then you should just leave your hand here for the day."

It was in moments like this that she didn't see a teasing look in his eye. Her body froze. Once again, he was able to pull off that almost natural tenderness that she just couldn't manage. Her heart twisted.

"Oh, yes, I suppose you're right," she sputtered, making him laugh at her again.

I sure would like to have several words with Lord Russel on the kind of advice he's been giving him!

This secret dispute must have appeared to Fiona's father and Hans as the banter of an intimate couple. They both saw her off with perplexed looks on their faces as she climbed into the carriage, mentally taking her anger out on Richard all the while.

The first day they went to the park, the second to Mrs. Bennett's shop. Yesterday was the teahouse, and today they were going to an art museum. Fiona thought it would be more effective for people to see them walking about town together, but Giles insisted on prioritizing Fiona's tastes instead.

"Are you sure about this?"

"Yes. I think more than enough people have seen us in the past few days."

"We certainly did get a lot of attention," Fiona agreed. She was pleased by this turn of events, seeing as she wouldn't have time to see any museums or galleries for the foreseeable future. She thanked him for his decision.

"You seem in good spirits today," he said.

"Do I?"

"Yes. I suppose it's because we're going to an art museum."

Perhaps that was indeed the reason. The members-only tearoom and the boutique they had visited were not the kinds of places Fiona liked to frequent. In contrast, art museums felt like home; simply entering one lifted her spirits. She nodded, her gaze dropping to the ring.

The turnout was nothing like the crowds downtown, but Giles's presence was enough to draw stares. He was a public figure, so it was difficult for him to avoid attention, even at the museum. The only difference Fiona noticed was that people stared in silent wonder at the sparkling ring on her finger. Some tried to talk to them, but Fiona and Giles walked right past them while they were preoccupied by the ring.

I never would've guessed it would have this kind of effect. Her finger felt heavy, but her heart felt light. Now she understood why Giles insisted on her wearing it.

Still, Fiona didn't feel that she could depend on the ring alone for their contract. The value of it was far beyond her means. *I wonder if I actually can get used to wearing it?*

She thought they would see the special exhibit and then leave, but Giles wanted to see the permanent exhibit as well. They moved to that floor, where there were far less people. Noticing how lightly Fiona stepped, Giles asked, "Do you come here often?"

"Yes. There are so many paintings here that I love. There are lots of other interesting things to look at too, not just the art."

"Like what?"

"Like the way that they hang the pieces. It can be a good reference for my work."

"How they hang the art?" He sounded curious, so Fiona suggested that he look at the paintings from the side.

Some venues hung paintings from the ceiling on a wire, but not this museum. Not a single metal fitting could be seen from the surface either; it was like the paintings were part of the wall. The painting before them at that moment was large and had an exquisitely ornamented frame. It looked heavy, but nothing indicated that the mount was insecure.

"There's no gap between the wall and the frame. You see how it's perfectly affixed from top to bottom? There are no obvious fasteners either. Mr. Roche says that he would like to be able to do the same at our gallery."

They couldn't use the method, common in homes, of affixing a string and hook to the back of the frame and then hanging it on a metal fixture. Strength and attractiveness came into question with such a method, but most importantly, the painting would bend forward at the top, drastically altering the viewer's impression. Roche hated that.

"It's easy to nail a frame into the wall, but the paintings at our gallery come in a variety of sizes. It wouldn't do if the foundation or holes left behind could be seen when we switch out the paintings."

"I see. I had never considered such a thing before."

"I can imagine why. Once a location is picked for a painting, it's rarely ever moved, right?"

Of course, the trick to how they exhibited the paintings at the museum was a secret. Roche and the other employees at the gallery had visited several times, trying to see if they could figure it out for themselves.

"So, how do they do it, then?"

"It's a trade secret," Fiona giggled, lowering her voice. "I'm sorry. It's just that it's a method for preventing theft as well. If we're contracted for it, though, we'll do it."

Giles looked disappointed, but he chuckled slightly, accepting her explanation.

No one was so unsophisticated as to try to insert themselves between the pair as they huddled close together, discussing the art in hushed tones. They moved on, looking at the remaining exhibits, until they neared the exit.

As they looked at the final painting, Fiona remembered something. She looked up at Giles. "I cannot tell you how they hang the frames, but I can tell you the secrets surrounding this painting." It depicted a brick-lined well, strewn with climbing roses. The artist was considered a master painter. It was the Platonic scene from a countryside, painted with gentle colors, and very easy on the eyes—a fitting piece with which to end the exhibit.

"It has a secret?"

"That's right. Normally, people just see this painting and go home. But..." Fiona paused as she placed her hand on his arm and began to lead him away.

They exited the museum and detoured to a quiet, narrow path along the right side of the building instead of the street directly ahead.

"Did you know that this museum has a small garden in the back?"

"No, I didn't."

"I only found it by accident myself. There's nothing leading people to it, nor any benches in it, so I doubt many people visit."

A variety of flowers grew in unorganized beds on both sides of the path, similar to how flowers might grow in front of someone's house. Fiona and Giles appreciated them as they followed the path. They came to a turn, which brought them to a small clearing.

"What have we here?"

"A small surprise for those who find this garden."

Surrounded by hard dirt was a brick well with a rope for hanging a bucket. Beside it was a bush of pale pink roses and carelessly stacked buckets. It was the same scenery they had just seen in the final painting. Even the flowers were near the same stage of blooming as in the painting as it happened to be the same season. The only difference was the angle of the sun.

"It really does look exactly like the painting." Giles smiled with admiration.

Fiona was glad that he was pleased by this discovery. "We're a bit too soon, but it won't be long before it looks exactly like that painting."

"Then let's come again in the evening next time."

"What?"

"I won't be available tonight or tomorrow night, but perhaps next week."

"You mean you want to come together?"

"Who else would I want to go with?"

Not many people knew about this garden, but it was a public area. He could come with anyone, anytime. But he had already decided to come again with her.

"Lord Russel?"

"No. If anything, we shouldn't tell him about this place. I have a feeling it would get overcrowded were he to start telling people about it. It would be nicer if it remained as tranquil as it is now, don't you agree?"

His unexpected response left her at a momentary loss for words. "Um, yes, I do. Thank you."

Why? What's gotten into me? Was the only reason she felt so happy truly that Giles showed he cared about a place she liked?

She looked away, full of emotions she couldn't possibly explain, and caught sight of the jewel upon her hand. It glittered brightly wherever she was, whether in the lighting of the store or outside in bright sunlight. She was sure that even when they came here next in the evening, it would look just as beautiful.

Come here? Again? She was surprised at herself to find that impatience at having to wait for that next time had taken root in her heart.

"Are you all right?" Giles asked.

"Oh, yes, everything's fine. Shall we go?"

"Yes, I suppose."

She hid her inner feelings as she turned with Giles to walk away. The fragrance of roses lingered in the air as they left the secret garden behind.

SIDE STORY

Getting Ready for a Party Is More Fun Together

I<small>T WAS THE NIGHT</small> of the ball at the Earl of Burleigh's estate and Fiona stood in front of her closet with her arms crossed. She was lost in thought over which dress to wear. "I've never been to a party at an earl's house before."

Her family had never been active in socializing with other members of high society. Normally, she attended only casual parties held by relatives or close acquaintances. Giles had said that the usual people would be in attendance, but his "usual people" were completely different than hers. Although the fundamental etiquette would be the same, there were sure to be unspoken rules that a woman like Fiona wouldn't understand. Fiona knew nothing of what they might be.

Now I really regret not asking Olga more about it. Olga spoke frequently about balls and parties. Unfortunately, the only thing Fiona could remember about parties at the Earl of Burleigh's estate was that they served good food.

Thankfully, she wasn't expected to be the belle of the ball. She expected that all she would have to do was blend in and not get in the way. But of course, Giles was one of the capital's most eligible bachelors. As his partner, she was likely to be the subject of severe scrutiny.

And most important of all, Caroline was the Earl of Burleigh's daughter. Considering the ardent way in which she habitually approached Giles, she was sure to display even more enthusiasm tonight. If Fiona looked like she did not belong next to Giles's side, it would damage the credibility of the rumors people were spreading about them.

"I can't stand around staring at my closet forever. Let's see, I wore this for the prince's celebration..." She unfolded her arms and started rifling through her closet.

She saw Caroline at that same party. It was unlikely Caroline remembered her, but she preferred not to risk anyone mocking her for wearing the same dress twice. *It'll be impossible for me to wear a different dress for every event, but this will be my stage debut, so to speak.* Unfortunately, she didn't have many options to choose from. Fiona owned a lot of clothes for a poor baron's daughter, but they were all everyday clothes that had been worn by her late mother.

Just as she was reaching for what she determined to be the safest choice, there was a knock at her bedroom door.

"Sister? Have you decided on what you'll wear—I knew it!" Cecilia marched into the room and put the dress back inside the closet.

"What are you doing?"

"I'll be right back." Cecilia sat Fiona down in front of the dresser and left the room.

"What's this all about?" Fiona was still confused by her sister's behavior, when she finally came back with a dress in her arms. It was a light blue dress that Fiona recognized. It had a cute design to it, which was why Fiona had given it to Cecilia.

"You said that you're going to a party at an earl's house tonight, right? And it's going to all be people you've never met before."

"Yes, that's right."

Fiona gave her a quizzical look. Cecilia grinned. "You're going to wear this dress. I made some alterations so that it fits you."

"What? When did you have time to do that?"

Cecilia didn't deign to reply, instead urging Fiona to stand up and undress. She ignored her older sister's bewilderment and deftly helped her into the garment. "Olga said that the women who attend those kinds of parties dress ostentatiously."

Olga was also close with Cecilia. They shared an interest in reading, so they often spent time together when Fiona was working. Fiona was not surprised that Cecilia talked to her about social events, but the way Cecilia phrased it made it sound like a bad thing.

"I suppose many of them do wear bright, beautiful dresses."

"And this is just a wild guess, but I suspect that the way you typically dress, Sister, is a bit, um, ordinary compared to them."

"Hee hee. Are you saying that I dress too plainly and you're trying to help me make up for it?"

"Uh...yes," Cecilia admitted awkwardly.

Fiona giggled again. She figured her sister must worry about her attending a party for higher-ranking nobles by herself.

She was grateful that Cecilia cared and allowed herself to be dressed up without any resistance.

When Cecilia was done and Fiona looked at herself in the mirror again, she was taken aback by the dress's appearance. "It looks so different than before." The big ribbon on the chest had been removed, and braided lace was embroidered along the hem. Cecilia had altered it to Fiona's tastes.

"Yes. And doesn't it look much prettier now?"

"You really did do a lot. It must've been so much work."

"Oh, it was nothing."

Cecilia was good with the needle, but surely it had been hard for her to get it all done for tonight. Fiona felt a complicated mix of gratitude and guilt. "But this was *your* dress."

"I'll just take it back when it's my turn to wear it. Besides, the color looks better on you," Cecilia said, as she handed over gloves as well.

"You even made sure to accessorize for me."

"And we're only just getting started." Cecilia was in high spirits as she sat Fiona down in front of the mirror and began to undo her hair.

"Wait, you're saying that even my hair looked too plain?"

"It simply won't do. We need to doll you up like never before for this party!"

"I don't think anything could manage to make me look very doll-like."

Fiona laughed at the improbability of it, but Cecilia appeared to be taking her task seriously. She must've been influenced by that novel Olga gave them, *A Downtrodden Lady's Beautiful Transformation.*

As if I could ever be transformed into a beautiful princess.

But as Cecilia fussed over her, Fiona realized that a small fraction of her nervous tension had left her body. It seemed that she had been more stressed over the imminent party than she realized. Cecilia was even more removed from high society than Fiona, but she had heard about what kind of person Giles was from her father, Hans, and even Norman.

Hearing about Giles must've worried her. And it's not like I can tell her it's all an act.

They weren't a balanced match in the least, but Fiona was touched at how, instead of saying a word about it, her sister was trying to make sure that Fiona looked her best. *Don't worry, Cecilia. I'll be fine.*

Having finished the final smoothing out of Fiona's hair, Cecilia set the brush down. Fiona looked completely unlike her usual self. "You should look your best if you're going to such a fancy party. I hope you have lots of fun."

"You're right. Say, Cecilia?"

"Yes?" Cecilia's reflection looked satisfied as they met one another's gaze in the mirror.

"Thank you. I never imagined I could look so pretty," Fiona said jokingly.

But her sister was extremely serious in her reply. "Oh, Sister, you're much prettier than you realize."

There was a pause before the two of them broke out in laughter.

PROFILE
Kobato Kosuzu

An author who mainly writes romance novels for women. Other works include *The Apothecary Witch Turned Divorce Agent* (DRE Novels) and *The Black Earl's Marriage Situation* (Amazaonite Novels).

The manga version of this work, *True Love Fades Away When the Contract Ends*, is currently being serialized through *Comic Ride* in Japan, and is also available in English from Seven Seas Entertainment.

TRUE LOVE Fades Away When the Contract Ends

One Star in the Night Sky